THE WORLD'S CLASSICS
THE KANTELETAR

THE KANTELETAR is a collection of lyrics and ballads based on Finnish oral tradition, first published in 1840–1. Its editor, Elias Lönnrot, intended it to be a companion work to his epic drawn from the same source, the *Kalevala* (also available in the World's Classics). Among the greatest poems in the *Kanteletar* are 'The Ballad of the Virgin Mary', a long sequence of legends from the Orthodox eastern Finns, and 'Elina', a historical ballad from western Finland about the burning of a young mother accused of adultery. The present selection from the *Kanteletar* is the first in English to appear outside Finland.

ELIAS LÖNNROT (1802–84) was a scholar and a district health officer covering a wide area of north-eastern Finland. In 1835 he published the first edition of the *Kalevala*, and in 1840–1 the *Kanteletar*. In 1849 he published the second and definitive edition of the epic, nearly twice the length of its predecessor. Towards the end of a prodigiously busy life, he began work on a new edition of the *Kanteletar*, but did not live to complete it. In Finland, a province of Sweden from 1155 till 1809, when it became a Grand Duchy of Russia, he was hailed as a national figure and is now regarded as the founder of literature in Finnish.

KEITH BOSLEY has published several collections of poems, most recently *A Chiltern Hundred* (1987), and a good deal of translation, including *Mallarmé: The Poems* (1977), *From the Theorems of Master Jean de La Ceppède* (1983), *The Kalevala* (1989), and *Camões: Epic and Lyric* (1990). In 1991 he was made a Knight, First Class, of the Order of the White Rose of Finland, for services to Finnish literature.

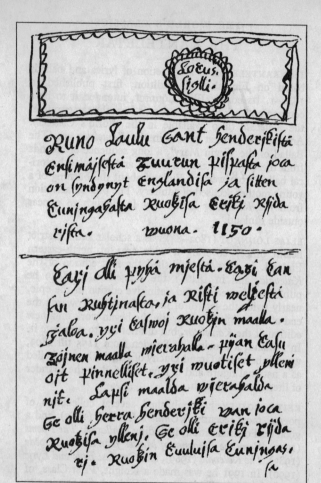

Locus Sigilli

Runo Laulu Sant Henderikistä Ensimäisestä Turun Pispasta joca on syndynyt Englandisa ja sitten Cuningahasta Ruotzisa Eriki ritsda ritsta. vuona. 1150.

Tämi olli pyhä mjestä. Tämi Tan sen Ruhtinasta, ja Risti weljestä zialoa. yri taswoj Ruotzin maalla. Zöjnen maalla mierahalla. pijan Tasu ojt pinnelliset. yri muotiset yllen nit. Lapsi maalda wjerahalda se olli herra Henderjeki van joca Ruotzisa yllenj. Se olli Eriti rijda ri. Ruotzin Tuuluisa Cuninjas. sa

'Seal here. Ballad about St Henry, first bishop of Turku, who was born in England, and then about the king in Sweden, Eric the Knight. In the year 1150. . . .'

First page of the oldest manuscript (c. 1671) in the folklore archives of the Finnish Literature Society, Helsinki. See poem 3:7.

THE WORLD'S CLASSICS

The Kanteletar

LYRICS AND BALLADS AFTER
ORAL TRADITION BY
ELIAS LÖNNROT

*Selected and translated from the Finnish
with an Introduction and Notes by*

KEITH BOSLEY

Oxford   New York
OXFORD UNIVERSITY PRESS
1992

Oxford University Press, Walton Street, Oxford OX2 6DP

Oxford New York Toronto
Delhi Bombay Calcutta Madras Karachi
Petaling Jaya Singapore Hong Kong Tokyo
Nairobi Dar es Salaam Cape Town
Melbourne Auckland

and associated companies in
Berlin Ibadan

Oxford is a trade mark of Oxford University Press

Translation and editorial material © Keith Bosley 1992
First published 1992 as a World's Classics paperback

British Library Cataloguing in Publication Data
Data available

Library of Congress Cataloging in Publication Data
Kanteletar. English
The Kanteletar : lyrics and ballads after oral tradition / by
Elias Lönnrot : selected and translated from the Finnish with an
introduction and notes by Keith Bosley.
p.   cm.—(The World's classics)
Includes bibliographical references.
1. Folk poetry, Finnish—Translations into English.   I. Lönnrot,
Elias, 1802–1884.   II. Bosley, Keith.   III. Title.   IV. Series.
PH329.A33   1992   894'.54110408—dc20   91-17132
ISBN 0-19-282862-2

Typeset by Cambridge Composing (UK) Ltd
Printed in Great Britain by
BPCC Hazell Books
Aylesbury, Bucks

Ei ilo iloitsijoille
ei remu remuitsijoille:
ilo ilman istujille
remu reunan katsojille.

No joy for those who rejoice
no merriment for merrymakers:
joy's for those who sit about
merriment's for onlookers.

CONTENTS

INTRODUCTION

'In literary poetry Finland lags far behind many other nations; but this need not greatly trouble us, for in folk poetry it is among the leaders.' The bold claim was made, not surprisingly, by a Finn, the scholar-physician Elias Lönnrot (1802–84), in the preface to his collection of Finnish folk lyrics and ballads, the *Kanteletar*, first published in Helsinki in 1840–1. A few years before, in 1835, he had produced the first edition of an epic based on heroic songs from Finnish oral tradition; the *Kalevala* was to be reissued in 1849, expanded to nearly twice its former length by the addition of spells and other material, to become the 'national' epic we know today. At 22,795 lines, the *Kalevala* was meant to stand comparison with the Icelandic collection of heroic songs, the *Elder Edda*, and more directly with the continuous narratives of the Homeric epics. After almost a hundred and fifty years, it has stood the comparison well, with translations into thirty-five languages (the latest being Hindi) and music inspired by it from a composer of international reputation.

Its companion volume, however, has not had the same international success. The *Kanteletar* has never been translated in full, and selections have appeared only in Swedish, German, Hungarian, French, and now English. The main reason for this is probably that epic is always special, whereas lyric is commonplace and ballad poetry widespread enough. Mid-nineteenth-century Europe was already acquainted with many collections of folk poetry that owed their existence to the Romantic concept of folk culture as a repository of national identity. Among these were Johann Gottfried Herder's *Stimmen der Völker in Liedern* ('Voices of the Nations in Songs', 1778–9), which first embodied the concept; the

German collection *Des Knaben Wunderhorn* ('The Lad's Magic Horn', 1805–8) of Achim von Arnim and Clemens Brentano, to be used by many composers including Brahms, Strauss, and above all Mahler; and the Serbian collections (1814–15) of Vuk Stefanović Karadžić. A general background to this aspect of Romanticism, together with an account of the Finnish tradition, is attempted in the introduction to my translation of the *Kalevala*. So without further preliminaries we will turn to the *Kanteletar*, which has also attracted composers, most notably Yrjö Kilpinen with his sixty-four *Kanteletar-lauluja* ('*Kanteletar* Songs', Op. 100) and Sibelius himself: the ballad whose tune he arranged for piano and the six poems he set are translated in this book, with details in the Notes.

The full title of the collection is *Kanteletar taikka Suomen Kansan Wanhoja Lauluja ja Wirsiä* ('The *Kanteletar*, Being Some Old Songs and Ballads of the Finnish People'). The word *kanteletar* (first syllable stress always) consists of *kantele*, the traditional zither-like instrument found among most eastern Baltic nations, plus the feminine suffix *-tar*, in Finnish folklore denoting a resident spirit; so *kanteletar* is roughly 'zither-daughter', a kind of muse. Here she is a lyric muse. Although the *Kalevala* describes the magical origin of the instrument and calls it 'a joy for ever' (*ilo ikuinen*, 40:234), the *Kanteletar* declares at the outset: 'no, music was made from grief / moulded from sorrow' (1:1). But this does not announce a sad book: it is merely a shorthand way of saying that what follows is lyric poetry.

There is debate among scholars about how far one can apply terms like 'epic' and 'lyric' to folk poetry, and indeed whether one can. I think one can and should: folk poetry is not produced by another species, and if such terms help us to map the territory, so much the better. But we must be on our guard against imposing alien categories, as when Petraeus, in the first Finnish grammar (1649), described the language in Latin terms—four forms of the ablative case, no subjunctive, and so on. When one approaches folk poetry from a literary angle, as a Western reader generally will, four terms are immediately problematic: 'poem' and 'poet', then 'epic' and 'lyric' already mentioned.

Most folk poetry is oral, passed from one generation to the next by word of mouth; the printed urban broadsheet was a rarity in Finland. In oral tradition, a poem or song (the terms are interchangeable) is a cluster of variants—recorded performances—on a single theme; if there was an 'original' from which variants have sprung, it has usually disappeared. It follows that there is seldom a poet as sole author: instead there were performers, who combined what they had learnt—most often from a relative—with their own contribution. Such a performer, of either sex, is called by the Finns a 'singer' (*laulaja*), but most Western languages have borrowed the more comprehensive Celtic term 'bard'.

Epic only means heroic, without reference to the length we associate with the former term: the longest epic text in the Finnish folklore archives runs to about 400 lines—an evening's performance—and there are countless much shorter epic texts. For this, the *OED* has 'epos', first used in 1835 (coinciding with the first edition of the *Kalevala*). No such inventiveness has been applied to oral lyric, probably because oral and written lyric are on a similar scale. But otherwise the difference is much greater: by its very nature, oral poetry is impersonal, even when—as often in lyric—it is in the first person. The balance between tradition and the individual talent, to which T. S. Eliot devoted a famous essay, is here weighted heavily on the side of the former. When the traveller Joseph Acerbi nearly 200 years ago heard a servant girl sing a variant of 'Missing Him' (2:43), he was wildly enthusiastic: 'It is nature's poet delivering the dictates of her heart in the words which love has suggested, and "snatching a grace beyond the reach of art." ' But she was not 'this Finnish Sappho', as he called her: she was a bard. The experience of Modernism has, paradoxically, made this ancient craft more accessible. *Je est un autre*, says Rimbaud; indeed, *Diversos modos sou* ('Diversities I am'), says Pessoa, giving us four poets for the price of one; and we may recall the babel of voices in 'The Waste Land'. But oral traditions like the Finnish are indifferent to such voices producing a variety of textures: all are subject to a single weave.

Hitherto we have assumed Lönnrot's texts to be genuine folk poetry; but are they? The short answer is no. As with the *Kalevala*, he reworked material that he and others had collected into a corpus, with which a nation could identify itself. In our passion for authenticity, we underestimate a process that may well have preserved many a national heritage. Did the author of *Gilgamesh* compose his epic on clay tablets? It is much more likely that it was assembled from oral variants. Homer remains a mystery, since a similar work of assembly seems to have been done before the Greeks had a form of writing that could cope with poetry. We are on surer ground with the biblical Song of Songs, whose grammar and vocabulary point to an Alexandrian compilation of love lyrics from a number of sources and periods, organized into a work of literature capable of wider interpretation, without which the lyrics would doubtless have been lost. A humble man, Lönnrot would have been horrified by such comparisons; but he too, in the timeless world of oral tradition, was at the coal face, bringing raw material to the literary surface. Since his labours, such a process has produced the Estonian epic *Kalevipoeg* and some Soviet 'national' epics—Abkhaz, Armenian, Kirghiz. So much depends on the editor (another problematic term, to replace which 'redactor' would be better, while Jean-Luc Moreau has dusted off 'rhapsode'): the Finns are lucky with Lönnrot, who made his papers available for anyone to compare his published work with the texts it is based on. From these it is clear that he respected his sources enough not to 'improve' them, though he allowed himself occasionally to add a poem of his own, based of course on his material: the poem quoted earlier (1:1) is such a poem.

Little wonder, then, that his name is absent from the title-pages of both the *Kalevala* and the *Kanteletar*, the founding works of literature in Finnish. (We are not concerned here with Finnish literature in Swedish, the language—ironically—of the 'national' poet Runeberg, who was a friend of Lönnrot.) Our elusive hero was the guiding spirit behind the formation in 1831 of the Finnish Literature Society, which has since published a million and a quarter lines of *Suomen Kansan Vanhat Runot* ('Old Poems of the Finnish People', 33 vols., Helsinki, 1908–48). From this monumental work an anthology with an English translation has been published as *Finnish Folk Poetry: Epic*; an anthology of lyrics is in preparation, which will show an international public the sources of the *Kanteletar*. Scholars have investigated the degree to which Lönnrot 'redacted' his material: it ranges from a standardization of dialect forms—the ballad 'Bishop Henry' (3:7) is little changed from the earliest manuscript in the Society's folklore archives—to 'new' poems like 1:1 or 1:174. A parallel might be drawn with Bartók's use of folk music: among his piano works, the *Sonatina* (1915) builds a classical form out of folk tunes, the *Fifteen Hungarian Peasant Songs* (1914–18) are a sequence divided into four movements, while the *Eight Improvisations on Hungarian Peasant Songs* (Op. 20, 1920) are separate pieces treating their sources more freely.

In a long preface, Lönnrot includes twenty-four 'later songs' composed since late medieval times, when Scandinavian influences moved in with the much older Finnish tradition, indeed one of the most archaic of known

European bodies of folk song. Most Finnish folk songs sung today are 'later songs', their foursquare tunefulness often finding counterparts in Western traditions: the ballad 'The Brother-Slayer' (iv) is an example. But the *Kanteletar* proper is devoted to that older, so-called Kalevala tradition, which survived longest in Karelia (eastern Finland and the Russian borderlands) and Ingria (south of the Gulf of Finland, in Russia). Its poems, in alliterative, astrophic trochaic tetrameter, were sung to simpler tunes built usually on five notes, corresponding to the five strings of the earliest kantele; the most characteristic rhythm was a five-beat bar of six short and two long notes. Sibelius uses this rhythm in the final section of *Rakastava* ('The Lover'), Op. 14. Examples of both 'later' and Kalevala tunes will be found in this book.

The *Kanteletar* is in three parts, which were first published separately. The first part, consisting of 238 'General Songs' with the preface, appeared in April 1840; the second part, consisting of 354 'Particular Songs', appeared in October 1840; the third part, consisting of 60 'Narrative Songs', appeared in March 1841. The three parts were first published together in 1864: they amounted (not counting the 'later songs' in the preface) to 652 poems, 22,201 lines. Towards the end of his life, after completing two long-term projects—a Finnish-Swedish dictionary and a collection of Finnish charms—Lönnrot returned to the *Kanteletar*. His plan was to produce a new edition, augmented with material collected since the first edition was published, rather as he had done with the *Kalevala* thirty-odd years before. He prepared a new third part, but did not live to complete the work. In 1887, three years after his death, the 'new' *Kanteletar* appeared. The old harmonious proportions were gone: the third part had increased by 77 poems and took up more than half the book. It had a mixed reception: creative spirits like the poet Eino Leino hailed

> Here a pretty Baby lies
> Sung asleep with Lullabies:
> Pray be silent, and not ~~~~
> Th' easie earth that ~~~~

But this is the other way round, an epitaph masquerading as a lullaby. We must return to the Finnish world, where poverty and child mortality were the norm: the bard Larin Paraske lost six of her nine children. Did mothers like her sing such lullabies to prepare themselves for the worst? Modern Finnish scholars incline to the less painful view that a mother wished her baby in another, better world, but the only language available was that which identified the otherworld as that of death. Whatever interpretation is offered, 2:178 is among the most poignant poems in the *Kanteletar*.

In one of the first folk poems to reach educated Finns—a variant appeared in the historian Henrik Gabriel Porthan's influential work *De Poësi Fennica* (1766–78)—a woman considers the advantages of being married to a man with a physical handicap, who is allowed to hunt on Sunday:

> The cripple's wife is well off
> the lame one's is laughing: yes
> the lame one catches the fowl
> and the halt pulls in the fish;
> he is not led off to war
> not dragged away to battle!

> (2:209)

Porthan and his students in Turku, the old capital, were aware of Ossian, whose cult was sweeping Europe; but they saw in James Macpherson, who in the 1760s had published texts allegedly translated from a third-century Gaelic epic bard of that name, a kindred spirit who nevertheless lacked the scientific approach to oral poetry which they were developing.

Masculine lyrics lack the resonance of feminine lyrics,

partly because men had epic songs, partly no doubt because they had less to put up with. But they also have something to say, as in the rueful boys' song about marrying a widow:

> A widow has had her games
> and spent a merry evening
> with her previous companion
> with her late husband.

(2:248)

War is 'a pleasant disease' (2:265) because it kills quickly—no finer feelings here—and a man will marry a bad wife rather than none at all, as a starving pike will eat a frog (2:314). Of the two singing matches in the collection, the longer (2:283) is given here. We are very far from the civilized affair of Western pastoral, but no nearer to the debate of the Provençal *tenso* and the French *jeu parti*, nor even to the exchange of insults in the Icelandic *senna* and the Scottish flyting. In the earliest Finnish *kilpalaulanta*, two shamans would compete in magic for power over a community. In canto 3 of the *Kalevala*, the young challenger goes down in the first round; in canto 12 we hear only the closing minutes of the match; in canto 27 the singers are so well matched that they resort to violence to settle the issue. In the rather less heroic *Kanteletar* poem, two poor, hungry shamans—or their successors—begin with boasts and end with threats; but the verbal play is as lively as ever:

> If I don't hear a singer
> or know him for a wise man
> I will sing him to a pig
> change him to a soil-snuffler.

'Wise man' renders *tietäjä*, literally 'knower' of secret lore, hence magician, wizard, shaman. In the Finnish Bible the word is used for the 'wise men' from the east in the Christmas story.

Magic plays an important role in the *Kalevala*, as a tool in a heroic world dominated by the spoken word: it ranges from the long narrative spell reciting the origin of iron in order to have power over it, followed by healing charms, which makes up most of the nearly six hundred lines of canto 9, to the six-line charm in canto 12 (373–8) to keep a dog from barking. Lönnrot put other charms that came his way into the collection already referred to, *Suomen Kansan Muinaisia Loitsurunoja* ('Some Ancient Charm-Poems of the Finnish People', 1880). As a result, there are no magic poems as such in the *Kanteletar*, though parts of—say—'The Ballad of the Virgin Mary' (3:6) might be used to bring good luck, as one might recite the *Ave Maria*. The omission was clearly deliberate: the book belongs to the lyric (and lyrical epic) muse, whose brief does not extend to such utilitarian matters as stopping blood.

And yet she incorporates that other workaday genre, ritual poetry. Ritual forms of words, from 'How do you do?' to most liturgy, are usually in prose; in the Finnish tradition, the most striking—Lönnrot said they made his hair stand on end—are the laments still screeched and sobbed over graves by old Karelian women on the Feast of the Dormition. But the heart of Finnish ritual is poetic, and Lönnrot, having given the *Kalevala* its fill in the wedding and bear-hunt cantos (19–25, 46), consigned the rest of his poetic material to the *Kanteletar*. In the wedding poems the division is between (broadly) the best man's party and that of the chief bridesmaid, without specifying the sex of the singer; but when someone of the latter party advises the bridegroom against giving his bride a black eye because people will talk (1:134) we recognize masculine humour, while the radiant praise of the bride's beauty from—of course— the same party (1:160) could come from either sex. Hunting rites, on the other hand, are purely *macho* until one returns home with one's prey: 'I go from men forestward / from fellows to outdoor work' (2:329) is the solemn formula of a man about to risk his life. (A lyric collected this century points out laconically that childbirth is just as risky.) In the present selection, the animal to be hunted is a bear, once sacred throughout the northern hemisphere and in some cultures too sacred even to be named, whence 'Beastie' in the rite that accompanied its dismembering (2:350). Here, as in canto 46 of the epic with its almost eucharistic ceremonial, we are in the numinous world of Sibelius' *Tapiola*, the tone-poem which evokes the domain of the forest-lord Tapio.

Lönnrot divided the sixty lyrical epic poems that form the third part of the 1840–1 *Kanteletar* into 'mythical' (*muinaisuskoisia*, literally 'referring to ancient beliefs'), 'historical', and 'legendary'. But the division seems arbitrary today—especially since the ten poems added in 1901 are unclassified—so it has not been used in this book. Besides, we need no such help in approaching some of the greatest poems in the Finnish language: here the *Kanteletar* reaches its full stature as a 'World's Classic'.

'The Ballad of the Virgin Mary' (3:6) is a sequence of six legends from Orthodox Karelia about Jesus' conception, his birth, the conversion of Stephen, Jesus' death, his resurrection, and his ascension into heaven. A fuller description in the Notes shows how widely the legends differ from what the original bards must have heard in church, even when allowance is made for the less rigorously defined teachings of Orthodoxy. Where the medieval English performers of the Mystery Plays were using texts written for them by local Church functionaries, the Finnish bards were interpreting Christian doctrine in terms of a pagan tradition. Following their example, Lönnrot adapted the first, second, and fourth legends in the closing canto of the *Kalevala* to depict the coming of Christianity to Finland. His principal source, in both the

epic and the *Kanteletar*, was Arhippa Perttunen
(1769–1840), a bard of Archangel Karelia who sang all
the legends except the third, that of Stephen, whose
horse will not drink water that reflects the star of
Bethlehem. Lönnrot inserted this from another source,
as any bard would have done if a theme took his fancy.
The result is what Lönnrot's exact contemporary Victor
Hugo would have called a *petite épopée*. Modern
Lutheran Finland refers to Arhippa's variants as 'The
Ballad of the Creator' or (on a German model) 'The
Messiah'; but Lönnrot was right to make Mary the
central figure, evolving from 'the holy, the tiny wench'
who gives birth to God—

> On Christmas Day God was born
> the best boy when there was frost:
> the moon rose, the sun came up
>   the dear sunlight woke
> and the stars of heaven danced
> and the Great Bear made merry
> when the Creator was born
> the most merciful appeared

—to 'the dear merciful mother' who brings about her
son's resurrection. She calls upon the sun to melt rocks
enough to let him escape from the grave—not so far-
fetched a notion where the ice melts only in May. But
without its ruler, the world is returning to chaos: in an
arresting image, the sun's behaviour is that of 'a headless
chicken' that runs and flutters about for a few moments
after decapitation. The sun, even so, does Mary's bid-
ding, and in contrast to the silent jubilation of the
heavenly bodies at Christmas (a mute echo of Psalm 19
rather than a choir of angels) we hear a sound like the
crackling thunder of a lake unfreezing:

> The Creator started from the grave
> the Lord awoke out of sleep
> got up on to the grave-side

climbed out of the pit;
and then the rocks sang with tongues
the boulders chattered with words
the rivers droned, the lakes shook
the copper mountains trembled
at the coming of God's hour
the Lord's mercy's unfolding.

The Kalevala tradition survived longest in the east, thanks to the tolerance of the Orthodox Church: indeed, it is to her parish priest that we owe the preservation of the astonishing repertoire—some 11,000 lines—of the Ingrian bard Larin Paraske (1834–1904), who greatly affected the young Sibelius. Further west, Catholics and Lutherans alike saw the tradition as purely pagan and tried to stamp it out, except when it could be made use of, as in 'Bishop Henry' (3:7). Finland's patron saint seems to have been an Englishman, who was murdered by one Lalli, the first Finn known to us by name. The ballad, composed to attract pilgrims to the saint's shrine at Nousiainen near Turku, shows the grim consequences of killing a bishop and putting on his mitre ('cap') and ring:

And the man to his sorrow
snatched the cap from off his head
and his hair tore off; he pulled
the ring from off his finger
and the flesh slid off.

Lönnrot's source is a seventeenth-century manuscript, a page of which is reproduced as the frontispiece to this book. In a later variant, collected at Vaasa in 1731, Lalli is finally portrayed 'skiing in hell'; Lönnrot's text, alas, draws the veil before that.

'Elina' (3:8), also from western Finland, may have survived because it does not invoke pagan heroes. It is regarded as the last great work of oral tradition in western Finland, from where it spread far: fragments

have even been found in Ingria. Its setting is the manor
of Laukko, near Tampere, where Lönnrot had his first
job as a tutor. Its heroine is a fifteenth-century peasant
girl who marries her landlord and falls victim to the
machinations of his jealous housekeeper. He has his wife
and baby burnt to death. As the fire takes hold, Elina
sends for her mother, who has seen the smoke and fears
the worst. She prepares to leave, clumsy in her haste:

> 'Woe is me, a wan woman:
> when I slip into my skirt
> it is always back to front.
> How is my daughter?'

A curse falls on the manor: the livestock 'all died with
straw in their mouths / perished at their oats'. Elina
undergoes an apotheosis, with 'a golden book in her
hand / the baby boy in her lap'. Her husband and his
housekeeper end up, of course, in hell: 'her plaits are
just visible / and her golden ribbons gleam'. Much of the
power in the Finnish tradition comes from such a use of
concrete detail to evoke states of mind.

Quite the nastiest poem in the *Kanteletar* is 'Palakainen' (3:25), which tells of a wife butchered by her
husband and served up to her visiting mother. The
source of the story is a Russian ballad (*bylina*) about a
certain Ivan Godinovich, who brutally murders a girl in
revenge for being mocked in a duel by her Tartar
betrothed. The purely melodramatic Finnish version is
included here because it vividly demonstrates the con-
struction of oral narrative from existing material: at least
six episodes have parallels in the *Kalevala* in utterly
different contexts. The food-praising formula 'I've eaten
a thing or two . . . but' is spoken in canto 17 by the
giant Antero Vipunen on swallowing Väinämöinen: we
know that much of a bard's skill—and an audience's
enjoyment—lay in the application of such formulas to a
variety of situations . . .

Altogether more palatable is 'The Thoughtful Dragon' (3:47); Lönnrot's title *Rangaistava sulho* ('The Guilty Swain') seems to miss the point of the story. The date is around 1500, when Swedish and Finnish church art was beginning to depict St George and the Dragon, and the south coast of Finland was under Danish attack. Scholars believe the poem was composed by a known but anonymous woman bard of south-west Finland, though Lönnrot collected the variant on which his text is based in the Ladoga area on the opposite side of the country, and another variant was found later in Ingria; the author surely deserves to be known as the Mistress of the Dragon. The poem, whose subject is unique to Finland, recalls the *Lysistrata* in that women unite in protest at the ways of men. The dragon is called upon to devour a girl who has been seduced and is therefore no longer marketable, but it refuses ('it sighed and it gasped', like the bride in canto 22 of the *Kalevala*) because girls, it says, become the mothers of soldiers to fight Tanumartti (according to the Ingrian bard, who thought that *Danmark* was somebody's name). Realizing that the dragon is on their side, the village women are going to string up the seducer, who is their St George. A Finnish dragon, by the way, is a *lohikäärme*, literally 'salmon-snake'.

The last poem in this selection is one of the seventy-seven ballads dropped after the 1887 edition, even though Lönnrot had contributed it to a *Festschrift* published in 1881 to honour J. V. Snellman, who had led the campaign to give Finnish equal status with Swedish in the emerging nation state. The original text, entitled *Turo, kuun ja auringon pelastaja* ('Turo, Rescuer of the Moon and Sun'), is therefore given as an appendix. The nearest *Kalevala* kinship is canto 49, where the final episode of the conflict between Kalevala and Northland is the latter's theft of the moon and sun and their recovery by the former; but the present poem—of Ingrian origin—is nearer to a general Arctic myth explaining the darkness of winter. The mysterious, Christlike Turo is an unexpected figure in the conservative world of oral poetry: after two unsuccessful attempts, he places the sun he has rescued to shine not only on 'those with fathers / the rich, the cherished', but equally on 'the fatherless / the poor, the beggars'. The poem was a judicious choice to honour the life-work of a great Finnish statesman; in the Europe of more than a century later, it forms a fitting conclusion to this book.

Certainly I must confesse my own barbarousnes, I neuer heard the olde song of *Percy* and *Duglas*, that I found not my heart mooued more then with a Trumpet: and yet is it sung but by some blinde Crouder [crowther, *crwth*-player], with no rougher voyce, then rude stile: which being so euill apparrelled in the dust and cobwebbes of that vnciuill age, what would it worke trymmed in the gorgeous eloquence of *Pindar*?

Referring in this famous passage from his *Apologie for Poetrie* to the Border ballad of Chevy Chase (No. 104 in the Kinsley *Oxford Book of Ballads*), Sidney reflects the attitude of our literary tradition towards our oral tradition. In most Western cultures, literary tradition has long been dominant: since the Middle Ages, talent has migrated to towns and got itself educated. In nations like Finland (the Baltic states, Hungary, Romania, Yugoslavia) this did not happen, and the chief vehicle of talent was oral tradition. Scholars speak of 'great' and 'little' traditions: for us, 'little' tradition means Percy's *Reliques of Ancient English Poetry* and its many successors, whereas the *Kanteletar* is 'great' tradition for Finns. A translator's job is to take his bearings in what might seem to be a topsy-turvy world, and to communicate gravity without losing the common touch. I have translated Lönnrot's text as literally as the considerable difference of idiom allowed, for Finnish is not an Indo-European language; the order of the poems is his, but most of the titles are mine. About half of the present selection was first published as *I will Sing of What I Know: Fifty Lyrics, Ritual Songs and Ballads from the Kanteletar* (Helsinki, 1990); some translations were first published by *Books from Finland* (Helsinki) and part of 'The Ballad of the Virgin Mary' was broadcast by the BBC World Service. The staff of this establishment's Reference Library have been courteous and efficient. A grant from the Finnish Literature Information Centre (Helsinki) added financial relief to poetic delight. Among those who have helped but cannot be held responsible for shortcomings that remain are Miss Senni Timonen of the Finnish Literature Society, who advised on the choice, checked the translation, and allowed me to draw upon her essay in the 1990 booklet; Academician Matti Kuusi, the late Professor Väinö Kaukonen, Mr Robert Layton, the Revd Tony Dickinson, Mr Anthony Rudolf, and my wife Satu Salo.

Upton-cum-Chalvey   K.B.

SELECT BIBLIOGRAPHY

In English

Matti Kuusi, Keith Bosley, and Michael Branch (ed. and trans.), *Finnish Folk Poetry: Epic. An Anthology in Finnish and English* (Helsinki, London, Montreal, 1977). Includes 'lyrical epic' texts on which ballads and a few other poems in the *Kanteletar* are based.

Keith Bosley (trans.), *The Kalevala, an epic poem after oral tradition by Elias Lönnrot* (Oxford, 1989; repr. 1990).

Lauri Honko, Senni Timonen, Keith Bosley, and Michael Branch (ed. and trans.), *The Great Bear: A Thematic Anthology of Oral Poetry in the Finno-Ugrian Languages* (Helsinki, forthcoming). Texts in fifteen languages, with English translation, introduction, and commentary.

In French

Jean-Luc Moreau (ed. and trans.), *La Kantélétar* (Honfleur, Paris, 1972). Versions of forty-eight poems, with an introduction.

In German

Erich Kunze (ed. and trans.), *Kanteletar: Alte Volkslieder und Balladen aus Finnland* (Helsinki, 1976). Versions of thirty-six poems, with the originals, an introduction, and commentary.

In Finnish

Elias Lönnrot, *Kanteletar, elikkä Suomen kansan vanhoja lauluja ja virsiä* ['The Kanteletar, Being Some Old Songs and Ballads of the Finnish People'] (Helsinki, always in print). The school edition of the Finnish Literature Society (Suomalaisen Kirjallisuuden Seura, SKS) gives the plain text of the first edition (1840–1), with Lönnrot's introduction and ten more ballads selected from the 1887 edition.

Väinö Kaukonen (ed.), *Elias Lönnrotin Kanteletar* ['Elias Lönn-

rot's *Kanteletar*'] (Helsinki, 1984). The text of 1840–1, with
Lönnrot's preface reproduced in facsimile, an introduction,
a history of the text, and a concordance.

Senni Timonen (ed.), *Näin lauloi Larin Paraske* ['Thus Sang
Larin Paraske'] (Helsinki, 1980). A selection, with notes and
an essay, from the repertoire of the Ingrian woman who was
one of the last great bards.

Toivo Vuorela, *Kansanperinteen Sanakirja* ['Dictionary of the
Folk Tradition'] (Helsinki, 1979).

THE SCANDINAVIAN TRADITION

The Brother-Slayer
iv*

Where have you been, where have you been
    my son, my merry son?
On the seashore, on the seashore
    mother, my darling one.

And what have you been doing there
    my son, my merry son?
I have been watering my horse
    mother, my darling one.

Why is there mud upon your back
    my son, my merry son?
Because my horse it swished its tail
    mother, my darling one.

Why is there blood upon your feet
    my son, my merry son?
My horse stamped with its iron shoe
    mother, my darling one.

Why is there blood upon your sword
    my son, my merry son?
I have stabbed my brother dead
    mother, my darling one.

Why did you stab your brother dead
    my son, my wretched son?
Because he dallied with my wife
    my dame, my darling one.

What now of you, where will you go
   my son, my wretched son?
To other lands, to foreign lands
   my dame, my darling one.

Where will you leave your old father
   my son, my wretched son?
O let him mend the parish nets
   my dame, my darling one.

Where will you leave your old mother
   my son, my wretched son?
O let her spin the parish threads
   my dame, my darling one.

Where will you leave your fair young wife
   my son, my wretched son?
Let her look on the parish men
   my dame, my darling one.

Where will you leave your little boy
   my son, my wretched son?
O let him bear the parish school
   my dame, my darling one.

Where will you leave your little girl
   my son, my wretched son?
O let her watch the parish herds
   my dame, my darling one.

When will you be returning home
   my son, my wretched son?
As soon as ravens glitter white
   my dame, my darling one.

And when will ravens glitter white
   my son, my wretched son?
As soon as geese are gleaming black
   my dame, my darling one.

And when will geese be gleaming black
   my son, my wretched son?
As soon as stones on water whirl
   my dame, my darling one.

And when will stones on water whirl
   my son, my wretched son?
As soon as feathers fall and sink
   my dame, my darling one.

And when will feathers fall and sink
   my son, my wretched son?
When the sun shines at dead of night
   my dame, my darling one.

When will the sun shine at dead of night
   my son, my wretched son?
When the moon scorches hot as day
   my dame, my darling one.

When will the moon scorch hot as day
   my son, my wretched son?
When stars are dancing in the sky
   my dame, my darling one.

And when will stars dance in the sky
   my son, my wretched son?
When all the world to judgement comes
   my dame, my darling one.

There is My Lover
viii

There is my lover, lingering
long at the golden court of the king.
    Ah my lovebird, ah my darling:
        now you do not come!

There are girls there whose looks entrance
but my love's eyes don't spare them a glance.
    Ah my lovebird, ah my darling:
        now you do not come!

Fair flowers, the summer morning is fair
but fairer my love's eyes, his air.
    Ah my lovebird, ah my darling:
        now you do not come!

The birds they sing from a lovely throat
but lovelier is my darling's note.
    Ah my lovebird, ah my darling:
        now you do not come!

Honey and cake are sweet on the platter
but my love's lips are a different matter.
    Ah my lovebird, ah my darling:
        now you do not come!

When shall I see that day of joy—
walking and talking beside my boy!
    Ah my lovebird, ah my darling:
        now you do not come!

Autumn is fast on the heels of summer
and yet my darling is a slow comer.
    Ah my lovebird, ah my darling:
        now you do not come!

Come, come, my darling, homeward, and hurry
or I shall die of longing and worry.
    Ah my lovebird, ah my darling:
        now you do not come!

The Weeper on the Shore

xix

I went for a walk of a fine summer night
in the vale where I once listened out for the light
    where the little birds warble
    the ptarmigans babble
and my heart looked about for some rest from its
                        trouble.

I cast my eye downward upon the sea side
and a fair young girl on the shore I espied
    who was sitting and weeping
    to see the waves leaping
and over the skyline sad vigil was keeping.

O why are you weeping alone on the shore?
Now still from your eyes I can see the tears pour.
    What sorrow and smart
    so pierces your heart
that even at midnight it will not depart?

She answered me: This is the torment I burn in—
that never again will that ship be returning
    which carried my lover
    the seven seas over
and left me to grieve and my poor heart to suffer.

For now I have waited a fortnight in vain
and there is no sign of his coming again.
    O what could it be:
    a dead man is he
or maybe a prisoner over the sea?

A little time more she turned seaward her head
and saw on the waves a small cloud glowing red
    but it was not a cloud—
    'twas her love's ship* that showed:
to earth's and heaven's Lord sing praises aloud!

Tunes of the three 'later songs' translated here,
as printed in the first edition of the *Kanteletar*. In the
first tune, the repeat signs and the last four bars may
be disregarded.

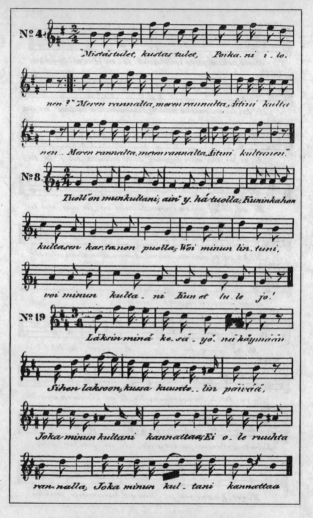

Some of the tunes to which poems of the
ancient Finnish ('Kalevala') tradition were sung, as
printed in the first edition of the *Kanteletar*. No. 1
(with many variants) was used in epic singing.

THE FINNISH TRADITION

LYRICS SUNG BY BOTH SEXES

My Kantele
1:1

Truly they lie, they
talk utter nonsense
who say that music*
reckon that the kantele
was carved by Väinämöinen*
fashioned by a god
out of a great pike's shoulders
from a water-dog's hooked bones:
no, music was made from grief
moulded from sorrow—
its belly out of hard days
its soundboard from endless woes
its strings gathered from torments
and its pegs from other ills.

So my kantele will not
play, will not rejoice at all
music will not play to please
give off the right sort of joy
for it was fashioned from cares
moulded from sorrow.

Why Not Sing?
1:4*

Even Lapland's children sing
 the hay-shod* pitch notes
 after scraps of elk
 flanks of small reindeer;
so why don't I sing too, why
 don't our children sing
 from a meal of rye
 from a well-stuffed mouth?

Even Lapland's children sing
 the hay-shod pitch notes
 when they've drunk a bowl
of water, bitten bark bread;*
so why don't I sing too, why
 don't our children sing
 from drink made of grain
 beer made of barley?

Even Lapland's children sing
 the hay-shod pitch notes
 from sooty camp fires
 from beds full of grime;
so why don't I sing too, why
 don't our children sing
 from bunks made of planks
 from rooms built of fir?

My Voice
1:6

I sang when I was younger
I banged my tongue when smaller
    but now I can't speak
    nor brag with my tongue:
    my tongue is poorly
    my tune very sick.

My voice has been much worn down
and my tune by a long yarn
    since last autumn, since
    the seed-time after:
a cough has closed up my mouth
and disease bolted my words
which once ran like a river
    sparkled like a stream.

    Yes, once my voice ran
like a ski across the snow
a boat on river-waters
a sailing-ship on the waves:
    now (poor me!) my voice
(wretched me!) my throat-trump★ is
like a harrow on burnt ground★
a felled pine★ raking hard snow
    a boat on dry rocks
a sledge on sands of a shore.

The Rate for the Job
1:12

Yes, I'd sing, practise my craft
but won't sing without money
wear down my mouth without gold
nor bang my tongue without cash:
a singer's palate grows tired
    a bard's throat dries up
when he* sings without money
when he warbles without gold.

    I would not ask much
    nor demand a lot:
a farthing,* the mouth opens
a penny, the tongue turns loose
a shilling for a whole word
half a shilling, half a word.

Or I'll ask for a swordsman
    for a saddled horse
for a king with his castle
    a priest with his church.

Plenty in the Larder
1:23

Come to us, dear Thomas;* bring
    Christmas when you come!
Come, All Saints,* hurry, Christmas,
    arrive too, Easter!

There's plenty in our larder
ready, lots of food laid in—
a haunch of cricket, a leg
    of gadfly, a rump
    of chaffinch, a frog's
little toe, a lizard's head!

The Calloo
1:25*

How do the lucky ones feel
and how do the blessed think?
This is how the lucky feel
    how the blessed think—
    like daybreak in spring
the sweet sun in the morning.

But how do the luckless feel
and how do the calloos* think?
This is how the luckless feel
    how the calloos think—
like a dark night in autumn
    a black winter day;
    I'm blacker than that
gloomier than an autumn night.

The Orphan
1:26

The calloo's spirits are low
swimming on the chill water
but the orphan's are lower
walking down the village street.

The sparrow's belly is chill
sitting on the icy bough
but my belly is more chill
as I step from glade to glade.

    The dove's heart is cold
as it pecks the village rick
    but I'm colder still
as I drink icy waters.

Heartbreak
1:42

The spruce's roots dry out, but
    my tears do not dry;
even the great seas unfreeze
but my sorrow will not melt.

    What can I, poor me
wretched me, what may I do
    with this great care, with
    this mighty sorrow?
Sorrow is breaking my heart
care is splitting my belly.

Should spring come again
should winter break off
perhaps, hapless, I'd die too
   break off, mean one, too—
leaf to tree and grass to ground
and me pining to the pit
   a grub to the grave
   wasted to the turf.

Better Unborn
1:46*

Better it would be for me
and better it would have been
had I not been born, not grown
not been brought into the world
not had to come to this earth
not been suckled for the world.

If I'd died a three-night-old
been lost in my swaddling-band
I'd have needed but a span
of cloth, a span more of wood
but a cubit of good earth
   two words from the priest
three verses* from the cantor
   one clang from the bell.

Cares
1:54*

Many rocks the rapid has
a lot of billows the sea
    but I have more cares
have been given more troubles:
more plentiful are my cares
    than cones on a spruce
beard moss on a juniper
    gnarls upon pine bark
    knobs upon a fir
    husks on a grass-top
    boughs on a bad tree.

No horse will be found
    between five castles*
    in six towns' earshot
that could drag my cares away
    carry off my griefs
    for no horse can draw
    no iron-shod jerk
without the shaft-bow shifting
the collar-bow shaking off
the cares of this skinny one
the sorrows of this black bird.

The Stifled Voice
1:57*

What has stifled the great voice
the great and beautiful voice
   ruined the fine voice
which once ran like a river
   sparkled like a stream
   rippled like a pool?

Grief has stifled the great voice
the great and beautiful voice
brought down the dear voice, so that
now it runs like no river
   sparkles like no stream
   ripples like no pool.

The Motherless Child
1:61*

The cuckoo in the spruces
has called and the bird has sung—
has called for others to hear
for the joy of the blessed
   but never for me
   has the cuckoo called
   since my mother died
the fair one who bore me fell.

Let a motherless child not
   let her nevermore
listen long to the cuckoo

on the sun side of a hill:
when the cuckoo is calling
    the heart is throbbing
    the heart is kindled
and the head bursts into flame.

Let a motherless child not
    let her nevermore
listen to the spring cuckoo
on the north side of a hill:
    tears come to the eyes
    waters down the cheeks
    flow thicker than peas
    and fatter than beans;
by an ell our life passes
by a span our frame grows old
when we hear the spring cuckoo.

A Plank of Flesh
1:72*

Whoever created me
whoever fashioned this wretch
    for this evil age
    with time running out
did not make me a word-smith
set me as a song-leader:*
better it would be for me
    and better it were
to be a song-leader than
    a footstep-leader
    a causeway on swamp
a plank on dirty places.

My great kin would, my
illustrious clan would wish me
to be a causeway on swamps
planks upon dirty places
somewhere to step on bad ground
a treestump on a well-path;
    they'd wish me to sink
in the swamp, fall on the rock
    be crushed in the dirt
    be jammed under roots.

But don't, my great kin
my famous clan, don't wish me
to be a causeway on swamp
planks upon dirty places:
a plank of flesh will not hold
a bone log is slippery
will not let a poor man pass
or the ill-shod pound across.

Home Sweet Home
1:75

Warm even a linen shirt
that's sewn by your own mother;
chill even a woollen cloak
that's made by a strange woman.

Warm mother's sauna
even without raising steam;
cold other people's sauna
    though steam may be raised.

Splendid home-baked bread
though it be full of corn-ears;
    bitter outside bread
though it be smeared with butter.

Woolly mother's lash
reedy father's whip
though it lash for long
though it whip for hours;
an outsider's lash draws blood
other people's is spiky
    though it strike but once
    or touch half of once.

Oh for precious home
darling life with dad!
    Though the bread was less
the sleep was more plentiful:
you weren't scolded for dozing
or cursed for lying in bed.

Don't Propose on a Sunday
1:88

A mother advised her son
a parent the one she'd fledged
as anyone those she'd groomed
herself brought into the world.
Thus I heard my mother say
    the old woman speak:
'My offspring, my younger one
    my child, my baby
if you want to wed well, to
bring me a daughter-in-law

don't propose on a Sunday
on the church path don't betroth:
then even a piglet shines
and even a sow wears silk;
the very worst concubines
hurry along the church path
all got up in blue stockings
all made up in red laces
    their heads bound in silk
    their hair tied in braids.

'Weekdays are the better time:
do your wiving then, my boy!
Take one from the threshing-floor
from those holding flails choose one
from those grinding betroth one
who has her coat on crooked
or straight without meaning it
whose kerchief has hoarfrost on
her bottom dusty from the stamper
her body white from grinding!'

The Court of the Birds
1:91

A poor man ploughed a field, both
    ploughed it and sowed it—
    sowed it with ten grains
    and ploughed ten furrows.
    There birds were produced
a lot of chaffinches grew:
    magpies cackled there
    and jays too chattered
    buntings went robbing
    and sparrows stealing.

A poor little willow-bird
    was espied, spotted
taking the last of the grain
snatching that most on the edge:
    it was bound, was wound
    it was lashed, was thrashed
it was beaten, was battered
it was trampled underfoot
and tears sprinkled from its eyes
blood from the troubled one's beak.
    It was brought to court
    set before the law.

The crane, the king of the birds
    himself sat as judge
the wild geese as jurymen
    the crows under oath.
The crane called out from his throat
    hooted from his neck:
    'Have you taken grains
from where a poor man has ploughed?'
The poor little willow-bird
    answering that says:
    'I've eaten two grains—
three would have been quite a lot.'

    The crane stretched his throat
to say over the table:
'Because you have taken grains
    and, wretch, been robbing
    where a poor man ploughed
    where he ploughed and sowed
there is no mercy for theft:
either your ears will be lopped
or your neck will be broken
    or your head chopped off.'

A swallow-bird, a small bird
spoke from the edge of the roof:
   'But you steal too, crane:
you take barley to live on
rye as much as you like, you
even bear off grains of oats!'

The crane gave out a great croak
   screeched an evil note
at the swallow, the smallest:
   'Have I been stealing
from where a poor man has sown?
I can live even without
   what a poor man sows.
I'll fly to gloomy backwoods
and there I'll rip off the rich
   break off crops of oats
or I'll eat forest berries
peck cranberries off a swamp.'

The swallow, the small bird said:
'As for me, I do not steal.
I am a joy to mankind
delight to all Christian folk:
I bring news of summer, I
bring about the warmer sun.'

The Crane and the Crow
1:100

A crane trumpets from a spruce
   a spindle-throat hoots:
'Disease, kill off girl children!

The berries are being picked
and the cranberries scattered!'

A crow cawed from a tilled field:
'No, Disease, don't kill off girls!
My wedding-meals would be lost.
A wedding is got from girls
and from wenches the best feast:
an ox is slaughtered for meat
a big cow struck down, one ox
for a wedding, two for fat
a heifer for sausages
and a sheep for extra meat;
    the guts are tipped out
the innards given to me
with my brood below the fence
with my family in the field.'

The Pan under Arrest
1:108*

From outside I heard singing
through the shingles statements made
    through the boards speeches
    through the moss-cracks words—
    a lament for booze
a song for the death of food
that booze had been put to death
    fair food had been lost
once among the crowd a joy
nourishment among the folk
the start of joy at evening
the start of grub at morning
good in the court of lords, the

best dainty in rectories
   fair in all places
   in farmers' cabins;
it consoled sorrowful hearts
   cheered up the tearful
it put sense into men's heads
and grub into people's hands
   it gilded eyebrows
   trimmed hems with silver.

Fie upon you, wretched pan!
What do you know of your deeds—
have you murdered, or stolen?
When you are under arrest
and firmly clapped in irons
when your lips are split apart
and your hat all torn, you are
like a squirrel on a bough
a cone turning in its mouth.

   Famous king of ours
majesty, lord of the land:
free the pipes under torture
all the pans from their shackles
   and set the pans free
   to be as they were
   to hang down by their
   handles and drip drops
   so that we poor boys
above the smoke-line* may get
   a goblet to grasp
a stiffener before us
   and make friends of foes
and good brothers of strangers!

The Origin of Beer
1:110*

I know of beer's Origin:*
    from hop beer was born.
    Hop, son of hubbub
was stuck in the ground when small
was ploughed in as vipers are
was tossed in as a nettle
on the bank of Osma's* field
down by Kaleva's well-side:
from it a seedling could rise
    a green shoot come up
on the bank of Osma's field
down by Kaleva's well-side;
it rose on a tiny tree
and towards the top it climbed.
So hop called out from the tree
and barley from the field-bank
water from Kaleva's well:
'When shall we get together
what time meet one another—
at Christmas, at All Saints, or
    only at Easter
    or this very day?
If only this very day!'

Then straight away they gathered
and came to one another:
a wagtail carried water
all the fleeting summer's day
    a red bird chopped wood
    a tomtit brewed beer.
That tomtit knew all about
and was good at brewing beer

but it did not know the name.
A cat spoke up from the hearth
a puss declared from the bench:
    'Beer is its right name—
a good drink for the well-bred
bad for those who've drunk a lot;
it makes the well-bred merry
    but makes the mad fight.'

The tomtit, the little bird
and the sparrow of small means
invited a lot of guests
to the beer worth drinking; 'twas
a good drink for the well-bred
bad for those who'd drunk a lot:
it put the mad in a whirl
the half-wits in a frenzy.
The tomtit, the little bird
and the sparrow of small means
    could not stay at home
but must flee to the forest.

The Dance

1:117*

The dance was not led by me
nor by my partner here: no,
the dance was brought from abroad
the caper led from yonder—
the White Sea of Archangel
the deep straits of Germany.
But no, not even from there—
    not a bit of it:
the dance was brought from further

the caper led from yonder—
from below green Viipuri*
   the great Finnish town.
But no, not even from there—
   not a bit of it:
the dance was brought from further
the caper led from yonder—
from beyond Tallinn, beyond
the outskirts of Novgorod
across St Petersburg's yards
and through Viipuri the green.

The doors of Novgorod creaked
the portals of Narva* mewed
the Finnish town's drawbridge dropped
the gates of Viipuri squealed
as the dance was led along
as the thing of joy was brought;
the horses drew it sweating
and the foals foamed as they trod,
water from the collar-bow
dripped, fat from the traces' tip
as the dance was led along
as the thing of joy was brought;
and the iron sledge clattered
the curly-birch strut thudded
the runner of birch rattled
the bird-cherry shaft-bow shook
as the dance was led along
as the thing of joy was brought;
   and grouse were moaning
on the sapling collar-bows
and squirrels were scurrying
along the shafts of maple
   black grouse were cooing
on the prow of the bright sleigh
as the dance was led along

as the thing of joy was brought;
the stumps leapt upon the heath
on the hill the pines pounded
the rocks upon the shore cracked
and the gravel moved about
as the dance was led along
as the thing of joy was brought;
the cows knocked over their pens
the oxen snapped their tethers
the women looked on smiling
the mistresses merrily
as the dance was led along
as the thing of joy was brought;
    and lords raised their hats
    and kings their helmets
    and old men their sticks
    and young boys their knees
as the dance was led along
as the thing of joy was brought.

The dance arrives in the yard
the joy under the windows:
    wait, I'll ask leave to
    lead the dance indoors.
    Whose leave shall I ask—
master's at the table head
the mistress's in the porch
the son's at the bench end, the
daughter's in the inglenook:
may I lead the dance indoors
the bird of joy to the floor?
The master uttered his word:
    'Lead your dance indoors
    lead your dancing-guest!
We shall kill the barren cow
for you all to pace the dance
and to play your game of joy.'

The dance slipped indoors, the joy
made its way into the room
stamping its feet on the steps
clapping its hands at the latch:
the stone oven moved about
the curly-birch post thudded
the floor of duck-bones rang out
and the golden roof echoed
    as the dance came in
as the bird of joy stepped in.

The Seduction
1:122*

    Evening, little bird
    evening, my treasure
evening now, my own darling!
    Dance, dance, little bird
    dance, dance, my treasure
dance, dance now, my own darling!
    Stop, stop, little bird
    stop, stop, my treasure
stop, stop now, my own darling!
    Your hand, little bird
    your hand, my treasure
your hand now, my own darling!
    Kneel down, little bird
    kneel down, my treasure
kneel down now, my own darling!
    Hold me, little bird
    hold me, my treasure
hold me now, my own darling!
    Hug me, little bird
    hug me, my treasure

hug me now, my own darling!
　　Kiss me, little bird
　　kiss me, my treasure
kiss me now, my own darling!
　　That's all, little bird
　　that's all, my treasure
that's all now, my own darling!
　　Get up, little bird
　　get up, my treasure
get up now, my own darling!
　　Farewell, little bird
　　farewell, my treasure
farewell now, my own darling!

Instructions to the Bridegroom
1:134*

　　Bridegroom, dear youngster
　　fair husband-to-be
　　don't hurt our maiden
　　don't you ill-treat her
with lashes don't make her squeal
with leather whips make her mew!
Never was the maid before
the maid at her father's home
with lashes made to squeal, no,
with leather whips made to mew.

Bridegroom, advise your maiden
advise the maiden in bed
and teach her behind the door
for a whole year in each place
　　one by word of mouth
　　two by a tipped wink

three by putting your foot down!
   If she doesn't care
   then, takes no notice
fetch a lash from the thicket
bring it under your coat hem
   to advise your maid
   and teach your charge with—
to advise between four walls
speak in a room caulked with moss
unheard by the village folk
no word reaching the village.
Do not bash her on the turf
nor beat her at the field edge:
the noise would reach the village
and the uproar the next house
the great row the forest, and
the wife's weeping the neighbours.

   And don't swipe her eyes
and don't box her ears: a lump
would come up on the eyebrow
a blueberry on the eye.
The village ploughmen would see
the village herdsmen would talk
the village magpies would slang
and the village women ask:
   'Has she been to war
   got mixed up in fights
or was she torn by a wolf
   or mauled by a bear—
or is the wolf your bridegroom
   the bear your fair one?'

The Bride Leaves Home
1:144*

I leave my swamps, leave my lands
   leave my grassy yards
   leave my white waters
   leave my sandy shores
to the village hags to bathe
and to the herdsmen to splash;
the swamps I leave to squelchers
   the lands to laggards
yards to those who run along
the fence sides to those who step
the wall sides to those who stand
the lane sides to those who walk
father's meadows to lynxes
to reindeer my father's fields
the glades for the geese to dwell
the groves for the birds to rest.

I am really leaving here
with another who's leaving
with another fugitive
going away from this house
   the hall father made
   brother's full cellar
to an autumn night's embrace
to a sheet of ice in spring
so there's no track on the ice—
track on ice, snowball on road
no footprint on the surface
on the crust no skirt's pattern
no hem's brush-mark on the snow
so mother may hear no sound
nor father hear me weeping

my tears of longing
my crying in bad spirits.

In Praise of the Bride
1:160*

Bridegroom, dear youngster
look at our maiden: she's like
a half-ripe cowberry,* or
a strawberry on a hill.
Pure is the bunting on snow—
purer is the one you have;
white on the sea is the froth—
whiter is the one you hold;
fair on the sea is the duck—
fairer is the one you keep;
bright is the star in the sky—
brighter is the one you wed.
You'd not have got from Savo*
nor brought from Turku either
nor found beyond Estonia
    nor fetched from Russia
    so fine a maiden
    such a bride as this:
her eyes are worth a blue one
and her cheek a crisp red one
her body a white paper.*

Herding Songs

1:173*

Where, O where is my good one
where does my dear one delay
    where does my joy sit
on what ground is my berry?
There is no sound in the glades
no noise of games on the groves
no music in the backwoods
no singing upon the knolls.

If my dear one were stepping
    my berry creeping
my own treasure were walking
my white one were wandering
my trump would blow differently
the slopes of the hill echo
the backwoods would start talking
    every mound singing
and the groves would be playful
and the glades ever joyful.

1:174*

This way my treasure has walked
here my beloved has been
this way my dear one has stepped
and my white one has wandered
here she has stepped in the glade
there she has sat on a rock.

The rock is much brighter, the
boulder better than the next
    the heath twice more fair

and the grove five times sweeter
and wild six times more flowery
all the forest more pleasant
because that treasure of mine
walked, that dear one of mine stepped.

1:186*

A fire burns on the island.
   Who lit the fire there?
A bridegroom lit the fire there.
What's the bridegroom toiling at?
He is adorning his sleigh.
   What is the sleigh for?
   It is for a maid.
What is the bride toiling at?
Cloth of gold she is weaving
of silver she is tinkling.

Children's Song
1:219*

What the thrush toils at
the partridge asks for
the hapless one takes
the troubled one steals
puts upon a spade
sets on a runner
hides under a door
shields with a bath-whisk.*

The farmer hammers
and tempers his spears
marries off his sons

hands out his daughters
in boots clogged with clay
in fancy mittens.

The sea-swell rumbles
and the wind it blows
and the king hears it
from five miles away
from six directions
from seven backwoods
from eight heaths away.

GIRLS' SONGS

Three Beauties
2:12

Summer is twice beautiful—
leaf on tree and grass on ground;
but I shall soon be a third—
    I a leaf waving
    I a flower heard of
    I a stalk swinging.

And yet I couldn't care less
a good stalk, about swinging
a good flower, about my fame
a sweet leaf, about waving:
the bad don't know of what's good
the mean of what's beautiful
clodhoppers of one ruddy
bumpkins of one red-blooded.

Churchgoers
2:20

    A tip-tap of shoes
a clip-clop of leather shoes:
the girls are coming to church
twinkling to the gallery.
They tear open their bosoms
    they wrench out their books

from which they intone a hymn
and read beautiful verses.

A clatter of clogs
a rattle of birchbark shoes:
the boys are coming to church
rowdily up the church hill
flasks of booze beneath their coats
jugs of beer under their arms.
The book is not in their minds
nor are the priest's best sermons:
in their minds the girls lie down
in their hearts they kindle fire.

Girl in Love
2:31

There's a certain one I know
a honey-berry* I like
a pet bird I'm attached to
a wild duck I hold on to
    who is keen on me
    and I'm keen on him.

He has lovely eyes
I have a warm heart;
he has not thrown me over
nor left me alone: he has
taken me to be his own
    called me his treasure
looked me out as his fair one
chosen me as his white one.

I'll hang on to him
   both hang on and swing
like a bird in a green tree
a squirrel on a spruce bough.

Missing Him
2:43*

Should my treasure come
   my darling step by
I'd know him by his coming
recognize him by his step
though he were still a mile off
   or two miles away.
   As mist I'd go out
as smoke I would reach the yard
   as sparks I would speed
   as flame I would fly;
I'd bowl along beside him
   pout before his face.

I would touch his hand
though a snake were in his palm
   I would kiss his mouth
though doom stared him in the face
   I'd climb on his neck
though death were on his neck bones
   I'd stretch beside him
though his side were all bloody.

And yet my treasure has not
his mouth bloody from a wolf
his hands greasy from a snake
nor his neck in death's clutches:

his mouth is of melted fat
his lips are as of honey
    his hands golden, fair
his neck like a heather stalk.

Little Bird
2:46

Where is my treasure
in what land is my berry:
is he on land or at sea
    on the mighty main
    or on Sweden's shores
in Germany's deep bays, in
    Jutland's cruel war
    the dreadful revolt
in which blood reaches the shin
    redness is knee-deep?

O who could bear news
    and who could fetch it
before others know my woe
and old women guess my care?
Make a pact, my little bird
a secret deal, my fair one
let us strike a bargain quick
and do a deal in secret
without the others knowing
or the next one noticing:
I will take care of your nest
provide food for your children
    and you fly meanwhile
    bring word to that land

where my treasure listens out
my leather-shod one looks out.

But a little bird has not
the strength to go over sea:
the small one will quickly tire
the weak one soon be breathless.
    Had the wind a mind
    and the gale a tongue
    it could take tidings
    it could bear him news
take a word, bring another
set an extra tongue astir
between two fair ones, within
earshot of two treasured ones.

The Warrior Bridegroom
2:47

Others' bridegrooms are at home
but my bridegroom is at war
my curly-head's on the move
my white-head is wandering
    out there in Turk-land
on Turkey's wretched borders.
There no mother can feed him
no Finnish sister brush him
and no Finnish girl kiss him:
he's been brushed by a smooth sword
touched by a war-sabre, given
a kiss by a big cannon.

Woe is me, silly daughter
that my bridegroom is at war

my matchless bridegroom at war!
I have both wept and waited
    spent my days hoping.
He promised to wed at home
to get married at Easter
but he did not wed at home
or get married in Finland:
he wed on the battlefield
vowed in a stranger's cabins
in a great lord's shelter, in
    a little lord's hut
with a pagan rod for priest
a strange power to hear the vows
    a straight sword for rings
    the bride a musket!

Irresistible
2:50

Should the one I know come now
and the one I've seen appear
    would I kiss his mouth
    open my jaws wide?

Come, come, little one I know
appear, little one I've seen
come, poor dear, to my cradle
and roll, darling, to my side
    to this new bed, this
    pallet spread with sheets!

If you'll not come, then don't come
if you'll not roll, then don't roll!
For I'll not call out, oh no

I shan't shout, I'm not bothered:
nature will bring you all right
blood will draw you to my side
your own blood will take over—
warm, it will make advances
        the sheets will serve us
the linen will unite us.

        Then, when you've got here
when you've come to my cradle
closer, closer, little bird
tickle, tickle, my treasure!

Elegy
2:53*

Long evenings full of longing
low-spirited my mornings
full of longing too my nights
and all times the bitterest.
I don't long for my supper
nor do I miss my breakfast
nor grieve for my other meals:
'tis my lovely I long for
it is my darling I miss
my black-browed one I grieve for.

There's no hearing my treasure
no seeing my marten-breast
no hearing him in the lane
driving below the window
chopping the wood by the stack
clinking outside the cook-house:
in the earth my berry lies

in the soil he's mouldering
under the sand my sweet one
beneath the grass my treasure.

Widow
2:55

Two fair ones were we
hens on this island
swans on the river
and looking alike;
hand in hand we walked
fingers interlocked
abreast in the kiln*
vying at the quern.
Two fair ones were we
and we were like chicks
till one went away;
the other greatly
grieves, weeps all her days
all the time pining.

I could still hope he would come
    just once hurry back
if he'd taken provisions
    eaten his farewell
    meal, gone overseas
to foreign lands found his way:
a man overseas comes back
but not one under the turf.

Brief Encounter
2:58

Two fair ones were we
hilltop refugees
among fine birches
among bright grasses:
now we are parting—
each one homeward bound.

Who could ever part
two fair ones at peace
sow hate between them
between two dear ones!
For two dear hearts God
himself cannot part.

Let her never in
a month of Sundays
be judged by the Lord
or behold his face
who stopped the one made
and snatched the one meant!

My own was springing
all my good sprouting
just forming a stem
bursting into bloom
but she came between
and snatched him away.

The Poor Man's Child
2:62

Oh, those laughable young men
oh, those silly simple boys
not finding the poor man's child
    at the creaking doors
    at the swinging gates
at the tumbledown fences!

    The poor man's child works
    spinning all the threads
    weaving all the cloth
and rocking all the children;
    the rich man's girl toils
at getting herself dressed up
has trouble from lying down
and more from sitting about.

The Three Suitors
2:70

Truly my mother
sang to me once as a child
    said I too would get
a bridegroom handsome, graceful
    black-browed and well-dressed—
said I would get him early
    after fifteen years.

    Fifteen years went by
the years went by, days rolled by

and my golden age went by
and my sweeter time rolled by
    and my fair day fled.

Then came suitors from three ways—
came as my mother had sung:
sorrow has given me rings
lamentation big kerchiefs
    and death will come third
carry me off to his home.

Daydreams

2:76

There's a certain one I know
a sweet stem I have in mind
a little man with red cheeks
a blond one with curly hair
and a Polish hat, fine boots
a woven hilt, a silk scarf . . .

Oh, if I had such a one!
Each day I would wash his head
each evening heat the sauna.
Water, bath-whisks I'd lay on:
water I'd bring from the stream
and bath-whisks from the thicket;
wood I'd gather from the wilds
though they were five miles away.

Oh, if I had such a one!
Then I'd have a little boy

and my hand would spin the wheel
and my foot would rock the child.

2:79

He's the one I'd wed
who had six gold belts
five skirts of broadcloth
who had six bedrooms
seven drawing-rooms
and eight cellars too—
cellars full of shelves
shelves full of barrels
barrels full of beer
to drink at my ease
for my tongue to lap.

If I got what I'm saying—
got into the drawing-rooms
I'd start being a lady
pet to a merchant
spouse to a rich man:
I would drink coffee all day
I'd stuff my mouth with sugar
and honey-cake as I like.

Against Gossip
2:98

Even if I were wretched
or were utterly stupid
they would call me worse, blame me
saying I was more stupid.

The big village is
full of mouths, still more of eyes
    even worse for ears;
but what do I care, madcap
a true wench, what do I fear
what's my concern with gossip
    my truck with rebukes?
I'm used to rebukes, I've been
the butt of village gossip
I've weathered village hatred
    I've been trapped by talk.

When I hear gossip
    or even slander
I will stand out more clearly
    hold my head higher
be like a stallion, or a
two-year-old pawing the ground;
    but should I hear praise
    or one compliment
I would hold my head lower
    and cast my eyes down!

Spinster

2:119

Look at others, the lucky
and the fortunate: they put
stockings on those meant for them
shirts upon those made for them.
But I shall never, luckless
I'll not in my lifetime put
stockings on one meant for me
a shirt on one made for me.

On my griefs I'll put stockings
a shirt on my low spirits
  all my ups and downs
  my switches of mood.

If I, luckless, could but die
and, wretched, be broken off
I would make stockings for Death
shirts for the sons of the grave—
  stockings from great griefs
  shirts from evil days
trousers from the cloth of care
  waistcoats from weeping.

The Victim

2:121*

When I was little I went
herding, a child driving sheep
I sat down among berries
fell asleep in a meadow.
From the thicket a stranger
from the birches a bounder
came and took what was my own
  possessed my good name.

I went weeping home
weeping to my father's yards:
he scolded from the window
my mother from her shed door
my brother from the gateway
my sister from the bridge end—
no refuge in the cabin
no mercy under the roofs.

Soon enough, poor wretch
  in these evil days
I'll find refuge in the wind
mercy among the billows:
I have a good mind to go
down below the deep billows
to be sister to whitefish
and brother to the fishes.

Do not you, my mother, then
    put water in dough
    from the broad bay end
without checking for tresses:
the water's full of my hair
the shores of all my tresses
of the hair of hapless me
of the locks of luckless me.

2:122

I, a little wench
like others bigger than me
bore a form upon my frame
developed supple hips; but
a dog came from the army
a frog from Savo's border
a bastard from Kuopio
some war-scum from Helsinki
    and he drank my blood
    possessed my good name
wetted my full-blooded face
    wore down my red cheek
    harassed my fair form
    bent my supple hips.

My poor mother did not know
and my father not at all:

he still treats me as a wench
she fusses me as a child
but I walk as a woman.

He knew all right, the bastard
the dog from the army knew:
he'd lain down below the fence
    he'd trampled the turf
    flattened the alders.

2:123*

My poor mother does not know
knows nothing of her daughter—
where the wench has been ravished
spoilt the one her mother bore:
'tis there the wench was ravished
spoilt the one her mother bore—
on a lesser island's side
on a leafy slope's border.

Once when afterwards I walked
    in that very place
the island itself declared
the island shores were mourning
and the fair turf was weeping
the dear shades were complaining
the young grasses were grieving
the heather flowers crying for
that ravishing of the wench
spoiling of the mother-borne
    and no young grass sprang
    no heather flower grew:
    they sprang nevermore
    on that hapless spot
where the wench was ravished, the
    mother-borne was spoilt.

Depression

2:124*

How do young maids feel,
the others, the lucky ones?
    This is how they feel,
the others, the lucky ones—
    like water stirring
or a ripple on a trough.
    But how do I feel,
    I, a luckless one?—
like hard snow under a ridge
like water in a deep well.

This is how I, luckless, feel,
    I, a luckless one—
as a horse up for sale feels
or a mare on the market
    or a bought stallion
    or a man who has
    killed, has felled two men
    has drowned two fellows.

2:127

    Cares don't come singly
    nor are cares twofold:
    no, cares are threefold
    sorrows manifold.
One care is upon my head
another under my feet
a third is at my midriff
    hunched under my heart.

The care that's upon my head
I could put it on my braid:
with a cord I'd fasten it
with a silk ribbon bind it.

The one that's under my feet
I could tuck it in my shoes:
with shoelaces I'd tie it
with my stockings block it up.

But the one at my midriff
if I strapped it with a belt
the belt just would not hold it
      and would snap in two
      for that midmost care
      it molests the heart
leads the tender to the grave
the young life to Tuonela.

Still, it would be bad to put
a bright eye under the sand
a fine figure in the soil
a fair face beneath the heath
for Death's maggots to rebuke
      the grave's worms to eat.

Grinding Song
2:137*

Mouth draws wolf into the trap
tongue draws stoat into the snare
will a maid into marriage
wish into another house.
      Grind, grind, young maiden

grind, young maiden's will
grind, hand and grind, foot
grind, mitten and grind, stocking
grind, grindstone and grind
a maid to a husband's house:
she has a mind for a man
smoulders for the village boys.
A boat's will is for waters
a ship's will for waves
a maid's will is for marriage
her wish for another house;
for a maid even at birth
a daughter is lulled
from papa's to husband's house
from husband's house to Death's house.

The Birch and the Bird Cherry
2:150

I was a bough on a tree
fostered by a lowly birch
in a naked glade
on land with no strawberries.

Next door a fair bird cherry
grew, a proud tree rose
on turf as thick as honey
on land the hue of liver.

With its bushy boughs
and its spreading foliage
it blocked the sun from shining
it hid the moon from gleaming.

Everybody looked at those
        and people admired
the handsome bird cherry's flowers
the blooms of the graceful tree.

But no one would look at me
        bother with a wretch
with the birch's humble girl
borne upon the lowly tree.

I grew yet a little more
        with my humble lot;
maggots gnawed the bird cherry
        destroyed its fair flowers.

The bird cherry felt a pain
        and was filled with care:
I remained standing
        with my small future.

Paying for the Milk: A Daughter
2:154*

How to pay for mamma's milk
make up for mother's torment
for the pains of my parent?
The happy, the lucky paid
        for her blood with cloth
for her labour* with velvet
but not among our brothers
nor among our sisters is
one to pay for mamma's milk
make up for mother's torment.
Pay with berries in summer

make up with birch sap?*
But berries pay for nothing
to offer for mamma's milk
and birch sap will not make up—
make up for mother's torment.
Shoot a swan on the river
on the stream a green-flecked fowl?
But that will not even then
     pay for mother's milk
make up for mamma's torments
no, not for my parent's pains.

Jesus, pay for mamma's milk
make up for mother's torments
Lord, pay for my parent's pains
all the cares of her who carried me!

Daughter-in-Law

2:155

The rower would like his boat
to run without rowing it
the grinder would like her quern
to turn without grinding it;
still more would the young maid like
once gone to a husband's house
to be in her father's home
beside her darling mother.

The maid in her father's home's
like a king in his castle;
in her husband's house she is
like a Russian prisoner.
Now I know how a serf feels
how a daughter-in-law feels.
The poor serf is not so poor
as the poor daughter-in-law:
he's a serf for a year,* she's
a daughter-in-law for life.

2:163

I grew at home like a stem
in a burnt-over clearing
I was not allowed to pound
    not wanted to thresh:
    serfs pounded, serfs ground
and strong hirelings threshed the grain.
    I lay in the loft—

in the loft behind a lock
underneath five woollen cloaks
on top of six pillows; I
went to the shed on the hill
   where I broke off wheat
   loaves, carved some pork
   sliced bits of butter.

I was married off
sold into a husband's house
got a harsh mother-in-law—
started on me straight away:
'Since you want to settle in
and live with mother-in-law
go to bed wretchedly late
get up woefully early
to shut the gates at evening
to open them at morning.
Turn the tubs upon their side
and tip the pails upside down
toss the cow its hay, the hay
of the cow that has carried
   snap off the lamb's straw
   and feed the poor calf!'

One night I'd been settled in
a single night I'd rested
and first thing in the morning
that evil mother-in-law
put a bushel in my hand
flung a sack of grain at me
   set me to grind it
   got me to pound it
ordered me to fetch water
wanted me to thresh the grain.
She came to look with a long
rowan in her hand, a stick

of aspen under her arm
   and she cursed hard twice
   she cuckooed three times:
'Devil where were you cared for
idiot, where were you brought up?
Sluts were cared for in secret
and brought up under a stump!'
Then she smote without warning
thrashed me with the rowan rod
beat me with the cook-house stick.

             2:171*

Big thanks to my bridegroom, I
bow my head to my treasure
who took me from serfdom, saved
me who was a serving-wench
snatched the cowlstaff off me, bought
me from running on the shore
pledged me from other folk's quern
   from the flail chose me.
Nor do I blame my mistress
run down my mother-in-law
   who bore such a boy
   nursed a white fellow
   for such a maiden:
luckless wench, I was always
   at other folk's quern
turning other folk's grindstone
and spinning other folk's wheel
wielding other folk's distaffs
and mending other folk's shirts—
   my own shirts got worse.

   I was always given
the thickest flail in the kiln
the sauna's heaviest brake*

the hardest club* on the shore
the barnyard's biggest pitchfork.
This is what I got to eat—
    bones from meat, fish-heads
    scratchings from roast pork
    crusts from loaves gone hard
    scraps from other meals.
No one believed me worn out
nor worried when I sank down
    though I groaned, weary,
    and tired, kept grinding.
More handsome ones grew weary
even stronger ones got tired
    let alone puny
me, a little tiny child.
Someone weak gets quickly tired
someone tiny's soon worn out;
    I too got worn out
when those fellows got worn out
    and I too sank down
when the horse's foals sank down.

Lullabies

2:174

Rock the child, rock the small one
    rock the child to sleep!
I will sing the child to sleep
wear him down to the dream-sledge.
    Come, dream, and hide him
    son of dream, take him
    to your golden sleigh
    to the silver sledge!

When he's got into the sledge
    snatched into your sleigh
drive along a road of tin*
    level copper ground
    take my tender one
    convey my precious
to a silver mountain ridge
to a golden mountain peak
and into silver backwoods
    to golden birches
where the cuckoos of gold call
    the silver birds sing.

2:178

    Rock, rock my dark one
    in a dark cradle—
    a dark one rocking
    in a dark cabin!

Rock the child to Tuonela
the child to the planks' embrace
    under turf to sleep
    underground to lie
for Death's children to sing to
for the grave's maidens to keep!

For Death's cradle is better
and the grave's cot is fairer
cleverer Death's dames, better
the grave's daughters-in-law, large
the cabin in Tuonela
and the grave has wide abodes.

2:179

    I rock, rock my son
    I swing my baby, to be

my prop in windy weather
my support in bad weather.

Rock, rock my small son
rock the man my son will be—
    one to plough, to sow,
    to scatter seed, to
lead the foal to the furrow
the black gelding to the glebe!

Rock, rock my small son
rock the refuge he will be:
he would only be a son
if he brought bread from the grove
a crust from the junipers
a red rind from the spruces
from the saplings a wheat loaf
to father for feeding him
to mother for suckling him.

Rock, rock my small son
rock the refuge he will be:
he would only be a son
if he built a new cabin
and put up a new sauna
before the cabin threshold
for the threshold a new door.

Rock, rock my small son
rock the refuge he will be:
he would only be a son
if he brought me a daughter
led one to carry water
got one to heat the sauna
who would soften the bath-whisks
    one to scrub my scalp.

2:182

A boy's good in the making
        fair in the breeding
in the having very sweet
in the swaddling fine, but I
as a mother do not know
as a wretched carrier
what will come of the one had
will grow from the one carried
whether the kin's doom has come
the curse of the clan has grown.
        Many such a dame
many a wretched carrier's
sought a prop from the cradle
a servant from her rocking
but a sharp-tongued boy has come
an ill-behaved son emerged—
        a tearer of hair
        scatterer of locks.

        A poor boy ought to
        think of the long run
        and not scold his dame
or answer his parent back.
If a son could see his tracks
and a child where he was born
        he'd not scold his dame
or answer his parent back:
he would obey his mother
and beware of his parent!

2:186

A boy's born, a burn* is born
a burn's born, a clearing grows;
a girl's born, a gap is born
a gap's born, a longing grows.

Who rocks a boy child
lulls something solid;
who rocks a girl child
makes for emptiness.

Cash comes from a lot of sons;
nothing from daughters, whether
married off to the village
   or brought up at home
   or killed by disease
   slaughtered at a stroke.

2:195

I rock this daughter
and this child I swing
lull my little-fingered one
   and nurse my baby.
   One day to this maid
   to this little girl
a bird-cherry collar-bow
will come, a birch shaft will drive.

One day to this maid
to this little girl
coins will come jingling
   little pence romping
   shillings capering
florins chasing each other.

One day to this maid
to this little girl
a Turku ring will be brought
other gifts from Tornio*
Riga silver rix-dollars*
and a ring cast in Finland.

One day this maiden of mine
    this little daughter
in a bright sleigh will be driven
    rowed in a red boat
to be spouse to a burgher
    pet to a merchant.

        (*for Miriam Rose Sherwood*)

The Weeper
2:204

There's nothing to do but sing
in the sledge of a good horse;
there's nothing to see but tears
in the bed of a bad man.
I have ended up somewhere
wretch, I have landed somewhere
beside one who hates me, up
against one who curses me:
now I have a strong harness
and a strong one for pulling;
now I have a handsome sleigh
and a handsome sleigh-burden.

I would always get along
    I would manage if
he who brought me did not scold
who caught me did not speak ill
who pulled me did not shun me!
But when he who brought me scolds
    who caught me speaks ill
    who pulls me shuns me
    I weep all my days
    and all my lifetime:

I weep my lovely eyes out
I roll my full-blooded face
   I drop my red cheeks
   my fair face I lose—
   weep the lanes crouching
   and the byres stooping
weep the tubs, weep the saunas
weep the wall joints in secret.

And now there is a river
   a clear shining sea
   from the tears I've wept
   let down from my head
   let go from my brow
   and dropped from my cheeks:
the women of my village
could bathe, so could those next door
thirdly the women at home
   and I too could bathe
   so could my parents
and my mother who had me
   in the tears I've wept
   let down from my head
   let go from my brow
   and dropped from my cheeks.

The Cripple's Wife
2:209*

   I grind, an old wife,
   mouldy-eared, I pant:
for me no daughter-in-law
grinds, no son's wife turns the quern
and my poor Jim does not grind

the lame fellow does not shove
    nor the crook-shank twist
my poor cripple does not rub.
I grind for my Jim myself
    twist for my crook-shank
    shove for my lame one
    for my cripple rub.

The cripple's wife is well off
the halt of foot's has it made:
the cripple has fed me well
    the halt on fishes
    Sundays fed on grouse
weekdays on game-fowl. Sunday
brings no ban on hunting, the
sabbath brings none on stalking:
always the merciful Lord
has given, the good God pledged
to the hunter Sundays too
to the seeker on weekdays.

The cripple's wife is well off
the lame one's is laughing: yes
the lame one catches the fowl
and the halt pulls in the fish;
he is not led off to war
not dragged away to battle!

Against Marriage
2:213

Don't, you podgy girls
don't, mother's children
ask hard for a handsome one

or choose a white one:
a handsome one's fist is hard
a comely one's whip is tough
a strong hand a white one has
a strong hand, a bad temper—
he'll eat your flesh, bite your bones
    draw fresh blood from you
share your hair out to the wind
    give it to the gale.

You girls, what's the fret
what's the matter with you maids
if for just a bit longer
you grow up at mother's home?
There is no care as a maid
as a girl no bad spirits:
    care is only nursed
    bad spirits put on
when the kerchief is fastened
and the cap set on the head.

Whatever kerchief's fastened
    curses will be got;
whatever cap is set on
bad spirits will be put on.
Trousers will be kept with care
a husband's clothes with trouble
    shirts with bad spirits
    stockings with great grief.

Three Children
2:220*

My mother reared, she
  reared a flock of hens
and another flock of swans;
she set them upon the fence
    stood them on the stake.
An eagle came, snatched them up
a hawk came and scattered them
the Devil came, dispersed them:
one he took to Russian soil
the next he brought to Savo
and the third he left at home.

The one he took to Russia
  was slain in a war;
the one he brought to Savo
in Savo a disease killed;
the third on home dirt will be
killed by eternal weeping
and by low spirits dispatched
and by hard days put to death.

How I Was
2:234

I was once as barley-land—
as barley-land, as oat-land
  as fair cabbage-land
as the best bean-field; but I've
ended up as mixed-crop land

somewhere to grow wretched hay
    I've become grassland
turned to a mossy hummock.

I was once (and how I was!)
    sweeter in my time
was a flower of six summers
lively as a five-year-old:
when I sat, the lands rejoiced
when I stood, the walls glimmered
when I danced, the heavens seethed
when I walked, the tree roots writhed.

I was a strawberry on a hill
a cowberry flower on a hillock
I cost marks as I lay down
and pence as I went my way;
but now I cost nothing, I
    don't cost an earthworm
dust eaten by a maggot
    old dirt from the kiln.

Against Widows
2:248

What took father's wits away
    which freak took mother's
promised me to a widow
to another's leftovers.

The Devil weds a widow
Death another's leftovers:
better to lie on willows
    rest on alder boughs
than upon a widow's bed
on a used woman's pillow.
Sweeter the side of a fence
    than a widow's flank;
softer the side of a grove
than a widow's beside is.

The Devil weds a widow
    the grave one twice wed:
a widow's hand is rougher
    than a dry spruce bough
with which she strikes the playful
    grabs the one who laughs.
A widow has had her games
and spent a merry evening
with her previous companion
    with her late husband.

The Devil weds a widow
disease one laid on a fleece:

flattened a widow's bed is
and a widow's fleece trampled.
    I'll catch a rock's speech
I'll hear a boulder's chatter:
    the rock will scream once
and the boulder will shriek twice
but a widow's jaws are locked
    her mouth shut right up!

Homecoming
2:258

I've trod Finland, the Islands
half of Ostrobothnia
a strip of Savo's border
both halves of Karelia★
looking around all the towns
sounding out Turku's castles
and nothing could trample on
my head, nor bring down my brain.

But when I came to home ground
one whore trampled on my head
another brought down my brain
and a third broke my breastplate.

Deceived
2:261★

Woe, woe, my hard luck!
My berry's been laid
my bird's been flattened!

If I knew who laid
   flattened my pet bird
he should lie down as a worm
slide as something in the grass
go as something like a snake
   as a lizard crawl.

If I knew who laid
   flattened my pet bird
better it would be for him
if he had lain on the earth—
on the earth as a black worm
   as a speckled snake
without rising from the earth
incapable of standing!

A Pleasant Disease
2:265*

The kin greatly grieves
   and all the kind mourns
   and the clan complains
that I am going to war
before the cannon's great mouth
into the iron churn's jaws
to sink in places of war
on paths of battle to drop.

But don't grieve, my kin
   nor mourn, my fair kind:
I'll not then sink in a swamp
   nor fall on the heath
   when I die in war
   fall in a sword-clash.

War is a pleasant disease
'tis pleasant to die in war
        sweet in a sword-clank:
a boy comes off suddenly
goes off without suffering
falls down without growing thin.

MEN'S SONGS

What Kind of Song?
2:271*

Well, brothers, we're still alive
dear brothers, drawing out tales
    on these poor borders
the luckless lands of the North.
    Brother, sweet of mouth
    sweet-mouthed mother's son
listen when I speak to you
    yes, while I'm talking:
    let's start off singing
    begin reciting—
you've a mouth and I've a mouth
and both of us a brave tongue!

    Brother, sweet of mouth
    sweet-mouthed mother's son
    this now I'll ask you
this inquire of the Dreamer:*
what kind of song shall we sing
which track shall we strike out on—
sing about that helpless year
that bad summer of the fire
    which burnt many lands—
many lands and many swamps?

I will sing of what I know
things I know and understand
things my old dame once told me
my own parent taught me when

I was a milk-bearded scamp
a curd-mouthed toddler.

A Singing Match
2:283★

CHALLENGER: Listen to this bard
study this singer: he is
a marvel to the hearer
a wonder to the idler!
When I get going in song
set about the work of tales
    I'll sing cairns★ to coins
    little stones to pence
    great mountains to tubs
of butter, cliffs to hen's eggs.

DEFENDER: When I get going in song
set about the work of tales
I will sing groves to bread-lands
    glade-sides to wheat-lands
    hills to rye puddings★
    little slopes to pies.

CHALLENGER: When I get going in song
set about the work of tales
I'll sing gravel to salt-grains
    the lake-bed to malt
    lake reeds to food-trees
lake rushes to cabbage-lands.

DEFENDER: When I get going in song
set about the work of tales
I'll sing the lakes to honey
    the lake sands to peas

> lake rocks until they glisten
> lake rushes till they are fair.

CHALLENGER: When I get going in song
set about the work of tales
I'll sing surf to rest content
the lake froth to settle down:
I'll sing the surf to pillows
    the lake froth to cloaks.

DEFENDER: When I get going in song
set about the work of tales
I'll sing the billows to perch
    white horses to whales
    lake depths to whitefish
    lake crags to salmon.

CHALLENGER: When I get going in song
set about the work of tales
I'll sing flagons from that land
    jugs from far-off lands
towards the russet table
on top of the long deal board.

DEFENDER: When I get going in song
set about the work of tales
I'll sing beer in the flagon
all the jugs full of honey
    the cups to brimming
the bowls up to the bulwarks.

CHALLENGER: When I get going in song
set about the work of tales
I'll sing the girl a pillow
the master a lynx-fur coat
the mistress a cloth mantle
and the boy a red waistcoat.

DEFENDER: When I get going in song
set about the work of tales
I'll sing pools upon the floor
in the pools blue scaups
their brows gold, their heads silver
all their toes copper.

CHALLENGER: When I get going in song
set about the work of tales
I'll sing the pools off the floor
the ducks to swamps, goldeneyes
to paths, swans to river-mouths
and the calloos to fence-stakes.

DEFENDER: When I get going in song
set about the work of tales
rocks will have lapped upon waves
gravels on waters floated
boulders will have boomed on heaths
cliffs flown into two.

CHALLENGER: When I get going in song
set about the work of tales
the very demons will sweat
the very gods get het up
with this child's singing
with my wretched cuckooing.
If I don't hear a singer
or know him for a wise man
I will sing him to a pig
change him to a soil-snuffler.

DEFENDER: What are you saying, poor thing
and why, sleepy, pestering?
If I want to draw level
and care to measure up, I'll
sing a branchy spruce base first

a shock-headed pine top first
    you wretch, down your throat
rascal, down your breathing-hole
so that your throat cannot drone
nor your breathing-hole rattle;
I'll sing the best of singers
into the worst of singers
ram rocks sideways in the mouths
jam boulders sidelong in those
    of the best singers
    the most skilful bards
mittens of stone on their hands
a stone slab on their shoulders
a cap of stone on their scalp
and on their feet shoes of stone!

The Singer
2:297

Others have been heard saying
    the village listens
to me, a thin one, singing
to me, a lean one, shouting
    singing a glad song
roaring out a merry one
    and many folk say
    a lot think that I
sing out of a wish for beer
    or for need of ale.

But I don't sing a glad song
don't roar out a merry one
nor out of a lust for beer
either, nor for need of ale:

I sing, lean one, for my cares
for my longings I am glad
grumble for my griefs, go on
for my days of suffering.

A bird was made for flying
one full of beer for shouting
one full of booze for whistling
one full of care for singing.

Marrying in Haste
2:314

There ought to be time in life
to choose a woman to wed
    to sound out a maid;
and yet a man willingly
knowingly marries a wife
    and brings home a scold
    a shrew for a mate
a fighter for company.

A pike eats even a frog
when it was swum far; a man
marries even a bad wife
when he has been long without.

Prayer against War
2:323

Keep us, steadfast Creator
  and guard us, fair God
from the hoofs of battle-foals
the trotters of war-horses!

Keep us, steadfast Creator
  and guard us, fair God
  from white iron's hoard
  the harsh blade's tip, from
before the big cannon's mouth
the jaws of the iron churns!

Keep us, steadfast Creator
  and guard us, fair God
  from great battlefields
from a fellow's killing-grounds
  where lead smites a man
  the tin ball hurls him
  where his head goes ill
  and his neck breaks too
  and his fine hair falls
  his locks come to grief!

Prayer for Peace
2:327

Old Man,* Lord above
O heavenly God*
bring peace to the border once

sweet agreement to Finland
peace to the poor borders, a
fair word to Karelia!

If you brought the border peace
good agreement to Finland
there'd still be a pleasant man
a sweetly-spoken bridegroom
    to plough and to sow
    and to scatter seed:
tears would not be heard in lanes
nor laments at ends of huts
groves would not spread to the turf
nor pine seedlings to the field.

The Bear Hunt

2:329*

The Old Man has sent fresh snow
    and the Lord fine flakes—
    an autumn ewe's worth
    worth a winter hare.
I go from men forestward
from fellows to outdoor work
on to the Old Man's fresh snow
flakes laid by the Worshipful
where there is no track of hare
    no ski-mark of mouse.

Take me, forest, for one of your men
for one of your fellows, Tapio
wilds, for your arrow-fetcher
mound, for one of your comrades;

take a man, teach him
to look up at heaven's arch
     observe the Great Bear
     and study the stars!

When you hear me coming, a
     real man stepping
     go pointing the path
     and blazing the trail
marking the sides of the path
straightening planks over swamps;
carve notches along the lands
slash a trail upon the slopes
that this fool may feel the way
this utter stranger may know!

     Lead a man on skis
by the sleeve, by the coat hem
push the left ski by the toe
and bring the pole by the joint
and bring him to that islet
     lead him to that mound
where a catch may be made, a
     prey-task carried out
     heads may be shared out
     portions divided
where spruces are in gold belts
     fir boughs in silver
     all birches with rings
     aspens in cloth coats!

2:332

What shall I put on
when I go to Forestland?
     I'll put on iron
     shut myself in steel

clothe myself in iron shirts
have steel belts made for myself.

> Then I'll smear my gun
> with black snake poison
> prepare my crossbows
> get my spears ready
> and say to my skis:
> A ski is foot-kin
> a spear is axe-kind
> a crossbow hand-brood.

> Great the ski that points
> good the leather-clad snowshoe
> great the sticky pine crossbow
> the spear-shaft from the north side.

2:333*

> Old forest greybeard
> golden forest king
> open now your shed
wide, dislodge the lock of bone!

Let a line of them run out
a row of them trot along
> down a golden lane
> down a silver road
where boards have been laid with silk
boards with silk, swamps with velvet
with broadcloth the slack places
the bad places with linen!

> Old Man, golden king
> silver governor
give me of your matchless ones
and bring me of your fair ones

jingling all with gold
clinking with silver!

Drive the game towards the slopes
towards the most open glades
on the days of my stalking
at the times of my prey-search!

2:350*

I thought it was the cuckoo
calling, the love-bird singing;
but it was not the cuckoo
    it was my own dog
at the Beastie's cabin door
in the bashful boy's farmyard.

My Beastie, my matchless one
honeypaw, my pretty one
    don't take it badly
if something occurs to us—
    bone-crunch, head-crack, our
    turn to scatter teeth!

Take off now, here, your head-dress
    and drop your snappers
    cast out your few teeth
    and move your quick jaws!

Serf and Master

3:4*

I will sing a tale or two
like wall timbers good and true
for masters, for mistresses
and for serfs who have no ease.

In Estonia was a serf
in boyar-land a herdsman.
    Bad wages were paid—
bad wages, his pains ignored:
the shortest cubit of cloth
    homespun gone mouldy
the smallest gallon measure
    and corn full of chaff.

Now, the serf was given leave
the serf leave, the captive power
to run home at Christmas, to
get away for the great feast.
The serf tumbles in soft snow
face in soft snow, head in clay
his fists in the bitter air
his bum on a bad bare patch;
    there the poor serf sank
and the wretched lackey died
    in his bare shirtsleeves
    quite without linen.
Three maidens of Tuoni came
and some dead were gathered up;
    the serf's soul was found

and the serf's soul was taken
   was led into heaven
brought into the hall of joy.

A silver door was opened
and flung wide a golden gate
   as the serf came in
and a silver chair was brought
a golden footstool borne up:
   'Sit on this, poor serf
   for you had, poor serf
   somewhere worse to sit
   when you were a serf
   lived as a lackey—
   to sit on hard wood
   or else just to stand.'

A silver flagon was brought
and a golden jug borne up
with honey, with mead inside
   and good-looking beer:
   'Drink from this, poor serf
   for you had, poor serf
but river-water to drink
   when you were a serf
   lived as a lackey—
to drink waters from a swamp
and dung-water off barnyards.'

   A little time passed
and that mighty master died.
Three maidens of Tuoni came
and some dead were gathered up
and the master's soul was found
the master's soul was taken
dragged to the cabin of grief

and cast into hell
the evil place of torment.

A fiery door was opened
and wrenched wide a tarry gate:
'Stand in there, mighty master
for you had somewhere to sit
 when you were master
 handing out orders—
 to sit in fine halls
 and in fair chambers.'

A fiery flagon was brought
and a tarry flagon snatched
 with fire, tar inside
 with lizards, with worms:
'Drink from this, mighty master
for you have drunk better things
 when you were master
 handing out orders—
yes, you drank beer when you sat
haughty at the table-head.'

'But why is this done to me
 to a wretched boy?'
'For this it is done to you:
you paid the serf bad wages—
 broadcloth gone threadbare
 homespun of no worth
 short cubits of cloth
 skimped across the beam
the smallest gallon measures
 and corn full of chaff.'

The master's soul was walking—
walking down a rocky road
down a rocky track he strode

a good two foot in his hand
a roll of homespun under his arm
silver in his grasp tinkled
and gold twinkled in his purse:
    'Come here, you poor serf!
I'll pay you the best wages:
    take from this, poor serf!'
'I will not take, poor master.'
    'Take, take, you poor serf
broadcloth instead of homespun—
    dozens of cubits!'
'I will not take, poor master.'
    'Take, take, you poor serf
    wheat instead of rye—
a bushel, not a gallon!'
'I will not take, poor master.'
    'Take, take, you poor serf
the best cow from my cowshed;
look out the best of my herd!'
'I will not take, poor master
for you gave none in your time.
You might have paid me on earth
rewarded in the big house;
you might have given wages
when I watered the cattle
watched over your flock of sheep
when I pounded your laundry
    and rinsed out your rags
when I clattered in the kiln
    boomed beneath the joists
and when on the threshing-floor
I wiped the sweat on my sleeve.
You thought the kiln was cracking
when my breastbone was cracking
you thought the beam was groaning
when my shoulder was groaning
you thought the joists were snapping

when my midriff was snapping
that the tall stack was slipping
when my blood was slipping out
   when I was a serf
   lived as a lackey.'

The Ballad of the Virgin Mary
3:6*

(i)

The Virgin Lady Mary
the dear merciful mother
decks herself, dresses herself
   fits on her head-dress
   puts on copper threads
   fastens belts of tin
and went out into the yard
tripping into the farmyard.
She looks out in the farmyard
listened out at the lane's end.
A berry called from the ground
a cowberry from the heath:
   'Come, maid, and pluck me
   red-cheek, and pick me
   tin-breast, and tear me
   copper-belt, choose me
   ere the slug eats me
   the black worm scoffs me!
A hundred have come to look
a thousand to sit about—
a hundred maids, a thousand
women, children unnumbered—

but not one would touch
me, pick luckless me.'

Mary, lowly maid
the holy, the tiny wench
went to look for the berry
and to pick the cowberry
     with her good finger-
     tips, with her fair hands.
She trod one hill, she trod two
till upon a third hill she
spied the berry on the hill
the cowberry on the heath.
So she went to the hill's tip
and she put this into words:
"Tis a berry by its look
a cowberry by its shape
too high to eat off the ground
too low to climb a tree for.'

She snatched a rod off the heath
from the hill a bent pine stick
with it brought the berry down;
the berry stops on the ground.
The berry rose from the ground
towards her fair shoe-uppers
and from her fair shoe-uppers
     towards her pure knees
     and from her pure knees
     to her glittering hems
rose from there to her belt-ends
from her belt-ends to her breasts
from her breasts towards her chin
from her chin towards her lips;
     on her lips it paused
then into her mouth it whirled
     swung on to her tongue

from her tongue down her gullet
then into her belly dropped.

Mary, lowly maid
the holy, the tiny wench
was fulfilled, was filled by it
 she grew fat from it:
 she bore a hard womb
a difficult bellyful
 for seven, eight months
 round about nine months
and by old wives' reckoning
 half of a tenth month.
 Her mother wonders:
'What's wrong with our Marjatta
and what's up with our home-bird
that she stays unlaced, always
slouches about unbelted
slops about without a skirt?'

(ii)

Now in the tenth month
 the lass feels a pain
 her womb becomes hard
her bellyful difficult.
She asked mother for a bath:
'Let me have a bath, mother
where a wretch may get relief
one in anguish may find help!'

Her mother indeed answers:
'There's a bath on the burnt hill
where a whore may have sons, a
scarlet woman bring forth brats—
 there in the whelps' nest
at the coarse-hair's manger-end!'

The wench is in a tight spot:
where to go, which way to turn
and where to ask for a bath?
She uttered a word, spoke thus:
'Piltti, least of my wenches
best of my hirelings, go now
for a bath in the village
a sauna at Saraja*
where, sick, I may get relief,
in anguish, I may find help.
      Go quickly, press on
for the need is more pressing!'

Piltti, least of her wenches
uttered a word and spoke thus:
'Who shall I ask for a bath
who shall I beseech for help?'
'Ask for Herod's bath, for the
sauna at Saraja's gates!'

Piltti, least of her wenches
      best of her hirelings
sprightly without being told
quick without being compelled
with her fists she grasped her hems
with her hands she rolled her clothes
      she both ran and sped
      ran to Herod's home:
the hills thudded as she went
and the slopes sagged as she climbed
pine-cones jumped upon the heath
gravel scattered on the swamp;
she came to Herod's cabin
and got inside the building.

Ugly Herod in shirtsleeves
is eating, drinking, feasting

at the head of the table
with only his lawn shirt on—
eats, drinks in the grand manner
    and he lives in style;
Herod declared from his meal
snapped, leaning over his cup:
'What do you say, mean one? Why,
wretch, are you rushing about?'

Piltti, littlest of wenches
uttered a word and spoke thus:
'I've come for a bath in the village
a sauna at Saraja
where one sick may get relief
one in anguish may find help.'

The ugly Herod's mistress
bustled at the floor seam, paced
in the middle of the floor;
she uttered a word, spoke thus:
'Who do you ask a bath for
who do you beseech help for?'
Piltti the little wench said:
'I ask for our Marjatta.'

The ugly Herod's mistress
    slams her hands down hard
    upon both her hips;
    she uttered, spoke thus:
'The baths are not free for all
not the saunas at Saraja's gate.
There is a bath on Tapio Hill
a stable among the pines
where a whore may bring forth brats
a scarlet woman have sons.
    When the horse breathes out
    bathe yourself in that!'

Piltti, littlest of wenches
    she both ran and sped
out of ugly Herod's home
    said when she got back:
'There's no bath in the village
no sauna at Saraja.
Ugly Herod in shirtsleeves
ate, drank at the table-head—
at the head of the table
with only his lawn shirt on;
he uttered a word, spoke thus:
"What do you say, mean one? Why,
wretch, are you rushing about?"
    I said with this word:
"I've come for a bath in the village
a sauna at Saraja
where one sick may get relief
one in anguish may find help."
The ugly Herod's mistress
bustled at the floor seam, paced
in the middle of the floor;
she uttered a word, spoke thus:
"Who do you ask a bath for
who do you beseech help for?"
    I said with this word:
"I ask for our Marjatta."
The ugly Herod's mistress
    slammed her hands down hard
    upon both her hips;
she uttered a word, spoke thus:
"The baths are not free for all
not the saunas at Saraja's gate.
There is a bath on Tapio Hill
a stable among the pines
where a whore may bring forth brats
a scarlet woman have sons.
    When the horse breathes out

bathe yourself in that!"
That's it, that is how she spoke
that was her only answer.'

Mary, lowly maid
the holy, the tiny wench
    still on fire with pain
in her hard belly-trouble
    put this into words:
'The time comes for me to go
as of old for the gipsy*
    or the hireling serf—
to go to Tapio Hill
to head for the lea of pines!'

She took a bath-whisk
for cover, begins to step
    she climbs the ache-hill
up the ache-mountain clambered
to the hut among the pines
the stall on Tapio Hill.
    Then, when she got there
    really arrived
    she says with this word:
'Breathe now, O good horse
sigh now, O draught-foal
over my heavy belly
    and waft some bath steam
    send a warm sauna
where, sick, I may get relief,
in anguish, I may find help!'

And the good horse breathed
    and the draught-foal sighed
over her heavy belly
    and what the horse breathes
    was made sauna steam

harmless water tossed—
'tis like steam being stirred up
like water tossed on hot stones.

Mary, lowly maid
the holy, the tiny wench
bathed her fill, bathed her belly
in all the steam she wanted;
and there she had her offspring
on the hay made in summer:
a boy was born at her knees
    a child on her lap.
On Christmas Day God was born
the best boy when there was frost
in a horse's hay-outhouse
at a rough-hair's manger-end:
    an ox spread out straw
a pig rooted up litter
to cover the little boy
to protect the Almighty.
On Christmas Day God was born
the best boy when there was frost:
the moon rose, the sun came up
    the dear sunlight woke
and the stars of heaven danced
and the Great Bear made merry
when the Creator was born
and most merciful appeared.

(iii)

Stephen is a stable-lad
in the ugly Herod's house;
he used to feed Herod's horse
    tend the stable-mount.
He took the horse to drink, the
covered gelding to the well
the blanket-back to the spring.

The spring splashed, the horse snorted
so Stephen the stable-lad
got down off the steed and looked
for something wrong on the ground
something wrong in the water;
saw nothing wrong on the ground
nothing wrong in the water.
'Why do you snort, raven's food
    and neigh, demons' horse?
There's nothing wrong on the ground
nothing wrong in in the water.'
'For this I snort, raven's food
    and neigh, demons' horse:
there's a new star in the sky
there's a speck betwixt the clouds.'

And Stephen the stable-lad
    cast his eyes eastward
    looked to the north-west
looked all round the horizon:
he saw the star in the sky
saw the speck between the clouds.
    So, a fox ran up:
    'Poor fox, wretched boy!
    You are fleet of foot
    a lively mover:
    go now, take a look
round behind the copper slope
why the star is born to us
wherefore the new moon has gleamed!'
    The fox ran and sped
    ran a long way fast
    ranged afar swiftly
round behind the copper slope.

    It meets a herdsman
and the fox put this in words:

'O my poor herdsman!
        Could you truly tell
why the star is born to us
the new star born in the sky?'
The herdsman put this in words:
'I both can and know how to:
why the star is born to us
the new star born in the sky
is because God has been born
the most merciful's appeared.'
        'Where has God been born
the most merciful appeared?'
        'There God has been born
the most merciful's appeared—
there in little Bethlehem
the son of God has been born
in a horse's hay-outhouse
at a rough-hair's manger-end
        on the rushy sedge
        on the frozen dung.
There God has given birth, the
Creator's laid his offspring;
he'd not exchange his baby
for copper to be melted
        for gleaming silver
        for glittering gold
nor for the moon, for the sun
        for the good sunlight.'

The poor fox, the wretched boy
        now came back from there
from behind the copper slope
bringing the news as it came:
'Why the star's risen for us
the new star up in the sky
is because God's son is born
the most merciful's appeared.

The Creator has laid his
offspring upon horses' hay
   on the rushy sedge
   on the frozen dung;
he'd not exchange his baby
for copper to be melted
   for gleaming silver
   for glittering gold
nor for the moon, for the sun
   for the good sunlight.'

And Stephen the stable-lad
took the horse to the stable
   tossed hay before it
laid on the broadcloth blanket
   fitted on silk girths
and went to Herod's cabin
   stopped in the doorway
stood at the end of the joists.
Ugly Herod in shirtsleeves
is eating, drinking, feasting
at the head of the table
with only his lawn shirt on;
Herod declared from his meal
snapped, leaning over his cup:
'Wash your hands, get at the food
   and feed Herod's horse!'

But Stephen the stable-lad
   put this into words:
   'Never in this age
not in a month of Sundays
shall I fodder Herod's horse
   tend Herodias' mount.
Let Herod feed it himself
   from this day forward
for a better birth is born

and a fairer power has grown.
    Now God has been born
the most merciful's appeared:
I've seen the star in the sky
seen the speck between the clouds.'

Herod declared from his meal
snapped, leaning over his cup:
    'You're telling the truth
    swearing without lies
only if this ox will low
and the blockhead will bellow
which is bones upon the floor
its flesh eaten, its bone gnawed
and its middle used as shoes
    all winter trod on.'

Well, the ox rose up to low
and the blockhead to bellow—
    rose to wag its tail
trample the earth with its feet
and Stephen the stable-lad
    put this into words:
'Now am I telling the truth
    swearing without lies?
    Now has God been born
the most merciful appeared?
For the ox rose up to low
and the blockhead to bellow.'

Herod declared from his meal
snapped, leaning over his cup:
    'You're telling the truth
    swearing without lies
only if this cock will crow
the son of a hen will screech
which lies roasted in the dish

meat smeared with butter
with its feathers fluffed
with its limbs stiffened.'

Well, the cock rose up to crow
the son of a hen to screech
     to rattle its bones
     to fluff its feathers
and Stephen the stable-lad
     put this into words:
'Now am I telling the truth
     swearing without lies?
     Now has God been born
the most merciful appeared?
For the cock rose up to crow
the son of a hen to screech.'

Ugly Herod in shirtsleeves
flung a knife down on the floor
     and says with this word
     snaps this reprimand:
     'You're telling the truth
     swearing without lies
only if the knife will sprout
which I've slammed down on the boards
and which for one year was carved
for two carried in a sheath—
     if the knife-shaft sprouts
     and it puts out shoots.'

Well, the shaft began to sprout
the shoots to break into leaf
     and six shoots sprouted
with a sweet leaf on each one
and Stephen the stable-lad
     put this into words:
'Now am I telling the truth

swearing without lies?
Now has God been born
the most merciful appeared?
For the knife-shaft is sprouting
which you slammed down on the boards
    and the cock has crowed
which was roasting in the pan;
and what's more, the ox has lowed
which was bones upon the floor.
Now I am leaving Herod
and fleeing the pagan's host:
I take my faith from Jesus
my baptism from the Almighty.'

That made the great man angry:
    Herod turned ugly
and he waged a fiery war
upon the Almighty's neck
and a hundred men with swords
a thousand iron fellows
rose to kill the Creator
to bring down the Almighty.

(iv)

Mary, lowly maid
the holy, the tiny wench
    concealed her baby
    she reared her fair one
underneath the grinding quern
and the gliding sledge-runner
under the siftable sieve
under the portable tub
and in her arms she feeds him
and in her hands turns him round;
she laid the boy on her knees
    the child in her lap

and began to comb his head
    and to brush his hair
    with a silver comb
    a gold-handled brush:
from her comb a tooth flew off
a bristle snapped off her brush.

She dashed off in search of it
    to find the bristle:
the boy vanished from her knees
the child from about her loins.
There the demons' gelding neighed
the evil one's horse snorted.
'Why, demons' gelding, do you
neigh, and snort, evil one's horse?'
'For this, demons' gelding, I
neigh, and snort, evil one's horse:
the boy's taken from your knees
the child from about your loins.'

    Mary, lowly maid
the holy, the tiny wench
because of that feels great pain
    and tearfully moans.
She dashed off in search of him:
she sought her little baby
her little golden apple
    her staff of silver
underneath the grinding quern
and the gliding sledge-runner
under the siftable sieve
under the portable tub
shaking trees, parting grasses
    scattering fine hay.
She sought her little baby
but did not find her baby
her little golden apple

her staff of silver;
sought him on hills, among pines
on stumps and among heather
checks out every juniper
through each patch of scrub she sorts
      checks out heather roots
and splayed out the boughs of trees.

She steps deep in thought
and she trips lightly along
      till she meets a road;
      to the road she bows:
      'O road, God's creature
have you not seen my baby
my little golden apple
      my staff of silver?'
But that road declared:
'Had I seen I would not say:
'twas your boy created me—
created for ill, not good
for a hard shoe to walk on
      for a heel to scrape
for every dog to run on
a steed to be ridden on.'

She steps deep in thought
and she trips lightly along
      till she meets a star;
      to the star she bows:
      'O star, God's creature
have you not seen my baby
my little golden apple
      my staff of silver?'
But that star declared:
'Had I seen I would not say:
'twas your boy created me—
created for ill, not good

to vanish in the summer
to be born in the autumn
to glimmer amid the cold
and to twinkle in the dark.'

She steps deep in thought
and she trips lightly along
    till she meets the moon;
    to the moon she bows:
    'O moon, God's creature
have you not seen my baby
my little golden apple
    my staff of silver?'
But that moon declared:
'Had I seen I would not say:
'twas your boy created me—
created for ill, not good
to go down in the morning
to come up in the evening
to wander alone of nights
    to shine in the frost.'

She steps deep in thought
and she trips lightly along
    till she meets the sun;
    to the sun she bows:
    'O sun, God's creature
have you not seen my baby
my little golden apple
    my staff of silver?'
The sun skilfully answered:
'I've both seen and heard of him:
'twas your boy created me—
created for good, not ill
to come up in the morning
to go down in the evening
    to rest at night-time

and to shine in the daytime.
Sure I have seen your offspring:
woe, luckless, for your baby!
    Luckless, your baby
    has been lost, been killed
the Creator weighted down
the Lord cut down and buried.'

(v)

    Now, we luckless sons
always think of other things
    babble about something
and are not even aware
    of the great God's death
the loss of the Almighty
when the Creator was killed
    the Almighty lost
    cut down and buried
the Creator weighted down.
    The devils tortured
the evil power troubled him
with a hundred spear-points, with
the blades of a thousand swords.
To a tree the Creator
was nailed, hung upon a cross
and there was slain; from the tree
the dead one was taken down
he was cut down, was buried
    in between two cliffs.
The mountains were pressed on him
the rocks were rolled upon him;
    a hundred swordsmen
a thousand iron fellows
    dragged them, eyes bloodshot
to the Creator's grave-side;
    a hundred swordsmen

a thousand bearers of shields
guarded the Creator's grave
watched over the Almighty.

The Virgin Lady Mary
the dear merciful mother
    she tearfully moans
    lamenting she groans
    she treads the road, steps
to the Creator's grave-side:
'Arise, Creator, from death
    and awake from dream;
rise while you are young from death
and while fair from being lost!
If you do not rise or wake
    soon I too shall come
    to die beside you
    to be lost with you.'
The Lord started in the grave
the Creator said, spoke thus:
'There is no rising from here
    as the wish is there:
rocks are beneath me, boulders
on top, along both my loins
with gravel against my heart
with sand against my shoulders.'

The Virgin Lady Mary
the dear merciful mother
    to the sun she bows:
    'O sun, God's creature
our fire the Creator made!
Shine for a moment sultry
another dimly swelter
for a third with your whole disc
    shine the boulders soft
    melt the rocks to salt

turn the gravel to water
    pour the sand to froth
free the Creator from death
wake the Lord out of the grave!'

    That sun, God's creature
    the sun, dear sunlight
flew as a headless chicken
as a fallen winged thing whirled
to the Creator's grave-side
the cell of the Almighty.
    A hundred swordsmen
a thousand bearers of shields
were set to guard the Creator's grave
watch over the Almighty
    and they ask the sun
they inquire of the sunlight:
    'O sun, dear sunlight
    why have you come here?'
The sun skilfully answered
    the dear sunlight said:
    'I've come near to look
    come close to observe
how the Creator was killed
the Lord cut down and buried.'

    The sun, God's creature
our fire the Creator made
shone for a moment sultry
another dimly sweltered
for a third with its whole disc
put the weary folk to sleep
    tired the pagan force
the young propped upon their swords
and the old against their staves
and middle-aged on their spears;
    shone the boulders soft

melted rocks to salt
turned the gravel to water
    poured the sand to froth
freed the Creator from death
freed the Almighty from loss.

The Creator started from the grave
the Lord awoke out of sleep
got up on to the grave-side
    climbed out of the pit;
and then the rocks sang with tongues
the boulders chattered with words
the rivers droned, the lakes shook
the copper mountains trembled
at the coming of God's hour
the Lord's mercy's unfolding.
The Creator rose from death
    and awoke from dream
dragged himself to a wet rock
on his belly painfully
    to wash off his blood
    to rinse off his gore;
    the sun, God's creature
our fire the Creator made
flew skilfully heavenward
    to its former place
    and freed men from sleep
    evil ones from rest.

(vi)*

The evil ones are forging
a shackle, preparing nails
to shackle the Creator
to lock him in iron locks
lest he should escape and flee
    and make off somewhere

from his grave that has been cut
from his pit that has been dug.
The Creator goes, he steps
and he walked a little way
heard slamming from the workshop
went there as a poor man, as
a beggar to the threshold.

Here the blacksmiths are forging
the demons' smiths are clanging.
He went to the smiths' workshop:
'What are the blacksmiths forging
the demons' smiths hammering?'
    That cruel Judas*
    worst of evil boys
and basest of father's sons
uttered a word and spoke thus:
'I forge a chain for the Creator
and a shackle-rope for God.
But I forgot to measure
how thick the Creator's neck
how thick and how long it is
    and how wide across.'
So the famous son of God
    put this into words:
'The Creator's neck is thick
    as thick and as long
    and as wide across
    as your own neck is.'

    The cruel Judas
    worst of evil boys
basest of father's sons said:
'How do you know the Creator's neck
how thick and how long it is
    and how wide across?'
So the famous son of God

uttered a word and spoke thus:
   'I was there as well
at the Creator's grave-side;
I looked round behind a stump
   rolled out of the scrub.'

   The cruel Judas
   worst of evil boys
basest of father's sons said:
   'Your jaw is as wide—
jaw as wide, your eyes as big
and your eyelashes as long
as these of yesterday's God
   the one we cut down—
   cut down and buried.'
So the famous son of God
   put this into words:
   'I have a wide jaw—
   a wide jaw, big eyes
and long eyelashes because
long I grew upon the heath
   grew behind a stump
and sheltered by a great rock.'

   That cruel Judas
   worst of evil boys
and basest of father's sons
uttered a word and spoke thus:
   'How very clever you are
more intelligent than most!'
So the famous son of God
   put this into words:
   'I'm very clever
more intelligent than most because
long I stared into the ogre's mouth
at the beard of who bites off.'

The cruel Judas
worst of evil boys
basest of father's sons said:
'The shackle would be ready
now, but I cannot measure
    this neck, my own neck—
how long and how thick it is
    and how wide across:
    my hand will not turn
    nor my finger fit.'
So the famous son of God
    put this into words:
    'If you will let me
    I could measure it
    for my hand would turn
    my finger would fit.'

That cruel Judas
    worst of evil boys
and basest of father's sons
uttered a word and spoke thus:
'If I let you measure it
do not lock it in the lock
don't press on the buckle-pin
    don't pinch in the tongs:
only the lock has been made
and no key has yet been got.
Locks are not unloosed with hands
nor bolts released with fingers.'
And he let his Creator
measure that neck, his own neck—
how long and how thick it was
    and how wide across.

At that our great Creator
    our God known to all
    measured, established

and he locked him in the lock
then pressed on the buckle-pin
    and pinched in the tongs.
He jammed the base in the cliff
kicked the butt into the rock
    to nine fathoms', to
    a tenth cubit's depth:
    'Now stay there, scoundrel
    and howl there, accurst
in the evil you have done
    the chain you have made!'

    That cruel Judas
    worst of evil boys
and basest of father's sons
now saw ruin coming, the
day of trouble arriving;
he let out an evil shriek
after that a dreadful roar
and a third one very loud.
And our great Creator, our
    God known to all said:
'Now shriek till the rock is hard
roar till the iron is harsh;
    stay there all your life
    dwell there all your days
till there is no moon, sunlight
no sun good to look upon
till there is no earth or tree
    nor men in the world!
    From this day forward
    may the rock be hard
    all iron be harsh
    the wind chill the sky!'

At that our great Creator
    our God known to all

rose into the air
above six bright lids
above eight heavens
towards the ninth sky
to where God the Father is
to the Almighty's chamber:
there he holds a court
judges all people
flings the evil to the depths
into frightful hell
and removes the good
leads them into heaven.

Bishop Henry
3:7*

Once two children grew:
one grew up in Cabbageland*
the other rose in Sweden.
He who grew in Cabbageland
he was Henry of Häme;
he who rose up in Sweden
he was King Eric.

Henry of Häme
said to his brother Eric:
'Let us go and christen lands—
in the lands without crosses
in the places without priests!'
King Eric said to
his brother Henry:
'What if the lakes have no ice*
the winding river's melted?'
Henry of Häme

said to his brother Eric:
'I'll circle Lake Kiulo*
go round the winding river.'

He harnessed the foals
bridled the yearlings
put the seats in the right place
set the struts in a row, threw
big rugs over the runners
small patterned ones at the back
and he drove straight off—
drove along the road, travelled
for two days in spring
two nights in a row.

King Eric said to
his brother Henry:
'Now we are getting hungry
with nothing to eat or drink
no stop for a bite.'
'Lalli is beyond the bay
the well-stocked on the headland:
there we'll eat and there we'll drink
and there we'll stop for a bite.'

Then, when they got there
Kerttu the idle mistress
banged with worthless mouth
slanged with idle tongue.
At that Henry of Häme
took hay for the horse
left pence in its place
took bread off the stove
left pence in its place
took beer out of the cellar
rolled coins in its place.
There they ate and there they drank

and there they stopped for a bite;
    and then they drove off.

    Now Lalli came home.
That evil mistress of his
    banged with worthless mouth
    slanged with idle tongue:
'People have been here:
here they ate and here they drank
and here they stopped for a bite
    took hay for the horse
    left sand in its place
    ate loaves off the stove
    left sand in their place
drank beer out of the cellar
    put grit in its place.'

A herdsman spoke from the post:
    'Surely you have lied!—
    Don't you believe her!'
But Lalli, the ill-behaved
and a man of evil kin
Lalli took up his hatchet
and the devil his long spear
and drove off after the lords.

    A faithful serf said
    a poor servant spoke:
'There is a thudding behind:
    shall I goad this horse?'
But Henry of Häme said:
'If there's a thudding behind
    do not goad this horse
    nor urge on this steed.'
    'What if we are caught
    or else even killed?'
    'Go behind a rock

listen from behind the rock
>   and if I am caught
>   or else even killed
pick my bones out of the snow
put them in an ox sledge, for
the ox to pull to Finland.
>   Where the ox grows tired
>   let a church be made
>   and a chapel built
for a priest to preach sermons
that all the people may hear.'

The evil man returned home.
The herdsman spoke from the post:
'Where did Lalli get the cap
the bad man the good helmet
the gallows-bird the mitre?'
And the man to his sorrow
snatched the cap from off his head
and his hair tore off; he pulled
the ring from off his finger
>   and the flesh slid off.

So to this ill-behaved man
who butchered the poor bishop
came the vengeance from on high
payment from the world's ruler.

Elina

3:8*

(i)

Elina, a young maiden
went to the shed on the hill

with a copper box under her arm
a copper key in the box.
'That's Klaus Kurki coming there.'
'How do you know that it's him?'
'I know the grim one by his coming,
the swing of his noble foot.'
'Are there no others as proud
as Klaus Kurki of Laukko?'

That Klaus came into the yard
with a hundred horsemen, with
a hundred saddle-fellows
the men with their golden swords
horses with silver headstalls.
Elina's five brothers sat
each one at the table-head
   and each one stood up
      went out to meet Klaus.

'Do you have a maid to sell
has a wench been kept for me?'
'No maid is sold on a hill
   traded at a farm;
horses are sold on a hill
   bone-hoofs at a farm.
But we have cabins as well—
one where a bridegroom may come
one to come and one to go.
We've a stable for horses
a hut for refreshing foals
a peg for hanging saddles.'

   That Klaus came inside
with his sword opened the door
and with his sheath pushed it shut.
'Do you have a maid to sell
has a wench been kept for me?'

The maid Elina's mother
    bowed to Klaus Kurki:
'Now, we have no maid to sell
    and no wench to hand:
    our wenches are small
    all of them half-grown.'
'There's that little Elina:
give me little Elina!'
'Oh, my mother, my darling
    don't give me to Klaus!'
'Little Elina cannot
    put a hireling to
    work, feed your household
    and tend your penned stock.'
'Nor is Elina needed
for the wench Kirsti is there:
I will let the wench Kirsti
    put the hireling to
    work, feed the household
    tend the penned stock too.'
'Yes, you have the wench Kirsti
who was mistress of Laukko:
she would burn me in the fire
    kill me with hard days.'
    'Kirsti has never
burnt anyone in the fire
    nor killed with hard days—
never has and never will.'

    Yet who is a fool—
    who but the poor wench?
If no fool, then short-sighted:
she took the gifts, gave her hand
and hand in hand with Klaus she
    went to Klaus's farm.

(ii)

Kirsti looked out through the glass
flashed a glance upon the panes:
   'O would that there were
someone to spoil that union
before I give up the keys
take orders from another!'

She went off to talk with Klaus:
   'O Klaus my darling!
   Little do you know:
Olaf has laid the mistress.'
'O my little wench Kirsti
if you can show to be true
what you've put into words, I'll
treat you still as you deserve
and burn Elina in fire.
   Five skirts of broadcloth
I'll give for you to walk in
before Lady Elina;
give the keys into your hand
before Lady Elina.'
   'O Klaus my darling
drive to the barn at Aumas—
the one called Little Meadows;
say you're going far away
staying many weeks at the
Ostrobothnia sessions.
And then I'll show to be true
what I have put into words.'
   Klaus promised to go.

'O my little Elina
slice butter into a box
lay provisions in a bag
   and a joint of ham
and a bushel of hen's eggs

for my long journey to the
Ostrobothnia sessions.'
   'O Klaus my darling
   don't linger long there:
the last weeks are with me, the
   very latest days.
Put your foot half down, let
others put the other half;
speak with half your words and let
others speak the other half;
drink only half a draught, let
others drink the other half:
so you'll get away sooner
from the witches of the North.'

Little mistress Elina
laid provisions in a bag
sliced butter into a box
   and a joint of ham
and a bushel of hen's eggs;
and Klaus drives away, but he
drove to the barn at Aumas—
the one called Little Meadows.

(iii)

   Kirsti goes washing
to scrub the little clothes, the
shirts of Lady Elina.
A din came from the cook-house
and the lady went to look:
'Kirsti, dear wench, why do you
make a din in the cook-house
and rattle where the pots are?'
'I'm rinsing a whore's garments
   a bad woman's clothes.'
   'Kirsti, my dear wench
   don't beat them so hard.'

But Kirsti thought of a dodge
and she beat them harder still.
   'Kirsti, bitch, don't beat
   my shirts so badly:
   they were not made here
but back in my mother's house.'
'Even good wenches are called
bitches, but not half the whores.
   It does not matter
   if, a poor hireling
   I am called a bitch
when great mistresses themselves
   have been with Olaf
on the long-bearded one's breast.'

Tears in her eyes, Elina
   came in from the shore.
Kirsti hurried after her:
   'O my dear lady
let us take the serfs off work
slaves from behind the oxen
and we'll have a little feast—
and a champion party too—
   as we used to do
when the master was away.'
   'Kirsti, my dear wench
   just do as you wish
as you did before I came;
tap all the other barrels
   but leave one untapped—
the one that was brewed for me.'

But Kirsti thought of a dodge
and she tapped that barrel first.
'Kirsti, my dear wench, you've done
one thing, I said another.'
'My dear lady, where shall I
make a bed for both of you—

in the new cabin
   above the main door?'
'No, not in the new cabin
   above the main door:
make it in Klaus's cabin
   as you used to do.'
'But 'tis full of guns that roar
   full of swords that flash
full of ravening iron
   of sharp steel weapons.'
   'Guns are death in war
   and swords in men's hands;
but they are harmless indoors
   fair in a chamber.
So make my night-bed in there
set out two woollen covers
   set out two pillows
   and two linen sheets.'

But Kirsti thought of a dodge
set out five woollen covers
   set out five pillows
   and five linen sheets.
Elina went to lie down:
   'Kirsti, my dear wench
you've not done as I said: you've
   set out five woollen covers
   set out five pillows
   and five linen sheets!'

Kirsti went from the chamber
   to Olaf's cabin:
   'Olaf, chief hired man
please come to Klaus's cabin!
You seem to be needed there:
they are calling urgently.'
'But what am I to do there?'
He went there nevertheless.

Kirsti hurried after him
   and locked the nine locks
and shot the tenth bolt; then she
ran to the barn at Aumas—
the one called Little Meadows:
   'O Klaus my darling
now I have shown to be true
what I have put into words:
Olaf's there even now, with
the lady in the chamber!'

(iv)

   Klaus rushed home forthwith
his head down, in bad spirits;
he struck a spark on tar-wood
kindled fire upon birchbark
thrust the fire in a corner
   lit the flame below.
The young Lady Elina
thrust her finger through the glass
with the wedding ring on it:
   'O Klaus my darling
   do not lose your ring
when you lose her who wears it!'

The wretched man Klaus Kurki
drew his sword out of its sheath
snatched the glittering iron
and slashed the finger straight off.
The young Lady Elina
held her child up to the glass
the weeper at the window:
   'O dear Klaus, darling
   don't burn your boy child
when you burn her who bore him!'
   'Burn, whore, with your brat

scarlet woman, with your child!
   That is not my son:
   it is Olaf's son!'

The young Lady Elina
called upon the Lord Jesus:
   'O dear Lord Jesus
merciful Lord Jesus, let
me see my mother again!
   May all places burn
but may this one run with tears
until I see my mother!
   Wat, my dear brother
run, oh speed to Suomela
   tell her to come here—
but say better than it is!'

   Wat went on his way
   he both ran and sped
quickly ran across the lake
and arrived at Suomela:
   'Aha, my dear dame!
The lady has summoned you.'
She got quickly out of bed
   and put on her clothes.
'Woe is me, a wan woman:
when I slip into my skirt
it is always back to front.
   'How is my daughter?'
   'Well enough, dear dame—
well before, but better now.'
'Woe is me, a wan woman:
when I pull on my stockings
they are always back to front.
   How is my daughter?'
   'Well enough, dear dame—
well before, but better now.'
'Woe is me, a wan woman:

when I step into my shoes
they are always back to front.
        How is my daughter?'
        'Well enough, dear dame—
well before, but better now.'
'Woe is me, a wan woman:
when I put on my kerchief
it is always back to front.
        How is my daughter?'
        'Well enough, dear dame—
well before, but better now.'

They came to Suomela bay.
'Woe is me, a wan woman:
smoke is rising from Laukko
        smoke from Klaus's farm.
What could they be doing there
        to make such thick smoke?'
        'Cocks are being killed
there, chickens being scalded
and sheep are being slaughtered
and pigs' heads are being scorched
to christen the little prince
celebrate the little boy.'

She arrived at Klaus's farm
and she went down on her knees
before her own son-in-law:
        'O my darling Klaus
take the boy out of the fire
the steady wife from the flame!'
'I'll burn the whore with her brat
and the harlot with her child!'
        'Don't burn her, dear Klaus;
let her go to other lands
        to conceal her tricks
to be ashamed of her deeds!'

Kirsti came running:
   'No, do not, dear Klaus;
   put in some bad grains
and a barrel of tar too:
   throw them in the fire
so that it may burn better.'
'O my little Elina!
   Ah, my poor dear child!
You might have curried favour—
curried favour with the whore.'
'Alas, my darling mother
there is not the slightest guilt
   nor the smallest blame
to fit an eyeless needle:
I did everything I could
and a little more on top.
   Now burn this place too
   because at the end
   before my harsh death
I could see my mother's face!'

She would have bidden farewell
   more, said a few words
more to her weeping mother
but at that moment the wretch
fell back, vanished among flames
   and sank in the blaze.
Thus she went, the young lady
Elina the young mistress
   who was fair of face
   fair in every way.
   You will be long missed
   and for ever wept
with ceaseless tears from Laukko
laments from Vesilahti.
Thus the end of the young wife
and of the little boy child.

(v)

Hardly half a month
or two weeks went by
when horses, a stableful
cattle, a byreful
all died with straw in their mouths
perished at their oats.
Klaus Kurki, the wretched man
the wretched and dreadful man
sitting on the shed threshold
was both sitting and weeping.
Jesus as an old man walked:
'Why do you weep, Klaus Kurki?'
'There is cause enough to weep
troubles enough to complain:
I've burnt my own spouse
set fire to my good armful
burnt my little son
and lost the one just carried.'
'I know Lady Elina . . .'
'Where is Lady Elina?'
'There is Lady Elina—
there in heaven's house
in the realm above
at the foot of the great God
before six candles
a golden book in her hand
the baby boy in her lap
Olaf at the door.
And I know Klaus Kurki too.'
'Where is Klaus Kurki?'
'There he is, there's Klaus Kurki—
in hell down below:
his spurs are just visible
and his feet glimmer below.
And I know the bitch Kirsti:

there, there is the bitch Kirsti—
    in the lowest hell
underneath the lowest gate;
her plaits are just visible
and her golden ribbons gleam.'

That Klaus drove away.
He packed his pipes in his bag
played going over the swamp
    echoed on the heath
boomed upon the lake; he drove
towards the unfrozen sea
below the deepest billows.
    Thus the young man went
and the married fellow too;
Kirsti as a cur behind.

The Fall of Viipuri
3:10*

Ivan the mighty master
our famous gold-buckled one
curries his war-stallion
    the rough-hair he grooms
    and says with this word
    and spoke with this speech:
'You would not weep, my mother
nor complain, hapless woman
if I were to go somewhere
to the yards of bold Sweden
    to great battlefields
to the killing-grounds of man.'
Mother tried to make excuse
the hapless woman to warn:

'Don't go to those lands
to the yards of bold Sweden
    to great battlefields
    to the killing-grounds of men!'

Ivan the mighty master
our famous gold-buckled one
    really meant to go
    promised to set out
put on one shoe at the hearth
the other at the bench edge
in the yard paces about
at the gates puts on his belt.
He lined up ships in the bay
    he prepared war-boats
and there are ships in the bay
    like great flocks of ducks;
he gave a thousand men swords
a hundred fellows saddles
mustered the men in his ships
    prepared the warriors
    as a scaup its young
as a teal musters its chicks;
    he erected masts
    fitted canvas-trees
hoisted sails upon the mast
    canvas on the trees
and there are sails on the mast
    canvas on the trees
    like a knoll's spruces
    or pines on a hill;
    and then off he sailed—
sailed one day on land-waters
the next day on swamp-waters
and a third on sea-waters.

    Now on the third day
he cast his eyes north-westward

saw the great Finnish castle
spotted Viipuri the green:
he draws along the waters
through the billows drives, landed
below the Finnish castle
below Viipuri the green.
He sent word to the castle
    pushed a paper in:
'Is there beer in the castle
and ale in the castle keep
    without brewing beer
    and sweetening malt
    for the coming guest
the arriving visitor?'
Matti son of Lauri, the
master of Viipuri spoke:
'Yes, there's beer in the castle
and ale in the castle keep
    without brewing beer
    and sweetening malt:
there's a barrel of hot rock
a pan of evil powder
    of tin mixed with lead
    a handful of eggs
    for the coming guest
the arriving visitor!'

Ivan the mighty master
our famous gold-buckled one
twisted his mouth, turned his head
and twisted his black whiskers.
He pushed a letter in haste
a paper in a hurry:
'Is there meat in the castle
and butter in Volmari*
without striking down an ox
    felling a great bull

for Ivan's supper
the Russian's tribute?'
Matti son of Lauri, the
master of Viipuri spoke:
'Yes, there's meat in the castle
and butter in Volmari
without striking down an ox
    felling a great bull:
a black gelding has just dropped
and a white horse has sunk down;
there's the carcass on a cairn
the skeleton behind the cook-house
for the great man's titbit, for
the murderous man's breakfast!'

Ivan the mighty master
our famous gold-buckled one
at that was angry, was wroth
very angry and furious
and he made his guns thunder
    and his cannon roar
and his open-throats bellow
    and his big bows twang
below Viipuri the green
and the great Finnish castle.
    He shot once, shot twice;
    he shot once—too low
    he shot twice—too high
he shot a third time—a hit.
And now the castle towers moved
    and the eaves rattled
    and the posts juddered
the stones of the castle swayed
and the towers came tumbling down.
    He shot once, twice more:
    the eaves rattled off

the shingles flew off
and the castle walls splintered.

Matti son of Lauri, the
shrewd master of Viipuri
put the keys of Viipuri
    on a golden plate:
    'Russian, my brother,
Karelian, my fine one:
    spare yet a weak life
don't shatter it with murder!
You've shot father, shot mother
    shot my five brothers:
    take gold in a cup
silver in a kilderkin
    to save my own skin
    to redeem my life!'

    Master Ivan, our
famous gold-buckled one said:
'Sweden's gold has gone rusty
Germany's silver tarnished:
I'll not care for your silver
nor ask, villain, for your gold
after you've made war on me
knocked the brains out of my head.'

Matti son of Lauri, the
shrewd master of Viipuri
    now took to his heels
    hurried to his ship;
he stepped aboard his vessel
    launched out on the sea
    splashing on the blue
with a woeful paddle's aid
    a crooked prow's help.
But as for master Ivan
our famous gold-buckled one

with leather shoes on his feet
so that the frost will not bite
   nor hard weather beat
he approaches the castle:
   the church is rubble
the castle an open space
the priest's cabin a few posts
and the priest himself shirtless
Sweden's fine one trouserless.

Katri the Fair
3:15*

Katri the fair, a young maid
and the prettiest of daughters
most fair even with no shoes
best even with no laces
even with no cap, no cloth
   as good as the rest
   goes late to the mill
at sunrise to the hollow.
She made a pact with the moon—
with the moon and with the sun
   that she would rise first
and Katri beat them to it:
   five fleeces she sheared
   rolled up six bundles
turned them all into homespun
into clothes she made them up
   before the sun rose
   the daylight came up.
She washed the big round tables
   the wide floors she swept
took her rubbish to the yard

and with her rubbish she stopped:
a noise comes from the village
a hubbub from the next house
    that of rich Riiko
    of the fat boyar;
it was a rattle of pans
and a clamour of stewpans
from the swamp a harness-clink
from the ice-hole shafts knocking.
    Katri ran to look—
and there is strong Riiko's son
    the fat boyar's son
    harnessing his horse
smartening his equipment
so that he may go wooing.
    Strong Riiko's son, the
    fat boyar's son said:
'Don't for any, fair Katri
except me, Katri the fair
put your head into a braid
    bind your hair with silk!'
And he slipped gifts in her purse
in her pocket stowed silver.

    She went weeping home
    wailing to the farm.
Her mother had time to ask:
'Why do you weep, little wench
fruit of my youth, why lament?
Go to the shed on the hill
put on a shirt of linen
one of hempen lawn on top
pull on a skirt of broadcloth
to go with your linen shirt!'
But Katri the fair, young maid
went to the shed on the hill

found a cord dangling
a rope's end swinging
and with it she brought about
her doom, met her death.

So who will carry the news
will tell it by word of mouth
to rich Riiko's house
the fat boyar's house?
A bear will carry the news
will tell it by word of mouth;
but the bear could not: it was
lost among a herd of cows.
So who will carry the news
will tell it by word of mouth
to rich Riiko's house
the fat boyar's house?
A wolf will carry the news
will tell it by word of mouth;
but the wolf could not: it was
lost among a flock of sheep.
So who will carry the news
will tell it by word of mouth
to rich Riiko's house
the fat boyar's house?
A fox will carry the news
will tell it by word of mouth;
but the fox could not: it was
lost among a flock of geese.
So who will carry the news
will tell it by word of mouth
to rich Riiko's house
the fat boyar's house?
A hare will carry the news
will tell it by word of mouth;
the hare said for sure: 'The news
will not be lost on this man!'

And the hare ran off
the long-ear lolloped
the wry-leg rushed off
the cross-mouth careered;
the hare ran and its head shook
its rump whirled, the field trembled
as it went to strong Riiko
    to the fat boyar.
To the sauna threshold it
ran, the sauna's full of maids;
to the kiln threshold it ran
on the threshold it squatted.

In the kiln is Riiko's son
    that fat boyar's son;
    strong Riiko's son, the
    fat boyar's son said:
'Put the hare upon the fire
    the squint-eye to stew!'
The hare manages to say
the hare certainly answered:
'Perhaps the Devil has come
    to stew in the pans!
I have come carrying news
to tell it by word of mouth.'

    Strong Riiko's son, the
    fat boyar's son said:
'What's the news to be carried
to be told by word of mouth?'
The hare manages to say
the hare certainly answers:
'Here's the news to be carried
to be told by word of mouth:
    Katri has fallen
the tin-breast has pined away
sunken the silver-buckle
the copper-belt slipped away.'

That strong Riiko's son
the fat boyar's son
seized his father's sword
honed it one day, honed it two
until at the third day's end
he asks and he speaks:
'Do you eat guilty flesh, drink
blood that is to blame?'
The sword followed the man's drift
it guessed the fellow's chatter:
'I eat if I'm fed
I drink if I'm given a drink.'

That strong Riiko's son
the fat boyar's son
went to the end of his field
pressed the butt into the field
turned the point towards the sky
turned himself upon the point
like a dry spruce bough
like a lopped juniper top
and with it he brought about
his doom, met his death
and said while he was going:
'Don't, bridegrooms to come
force another man's daughter
to marry against her will!'

Hannus Pannus

3:16*

Hannus Pannus, handsome man
went off to the Falls to woo
the Brook's youngest girl
the boyar's best child

and he said when he got there
   and reached the boyar:
'The best for me, not the worst
tallest for me, not shortest!'
   The Brook's youngest girl
and the boyar's best child said:
'Neither the best nor the worst
neither tallest nor shortest
for you have a wedded wife
a mistress* in residence.
   Kill your wedded wife
murder the mistress you have!'

Hannus Pannus, handsome man
   trusted a whore's lures
an evil woman's temptings
leapt on the two-year's withers
mounted the white-face's flanks
   and he went straight home
   killed his wedded wife
murdered the mistress he had.
He went to the Falls to woo
   the Brook's youngest girl
   the boyar's best child
and he said when he'd gone there:
'The best for me, not the worst
tallest for me, not shortest!'
   The Brook's youngest girl
and the boyar's best child said:
'Neither the best nor the worst
neither tallest nor shortest
for you've killed your wedded wife
murdered the mistress you had:
   you might kill me too
slay someone of good family
and then go buy a new one
   soon woo number three!'

Palakainen
3:25*

A maid sat on a quay end
sang from the planks of the quay:
'Swanlike* born, swanlike I grew
swanlike I have lived my time.
If I married Joukonen
    swanlike he'd keep me
workless, beltless, mittenless
    swanlike he'd feed me
he'd give me river-water
to drink, damp me with horsetails
    bring me to sedges
    leave me on the hay
with a big rock for shelter
    tucked under a cliff.'

    Jouko chanced to hear
as he stood below the wall:
    where he heard, he wooed
    where he wooed, he pledged
    where he pledged, he took.
He knocked at Kommi's window
    wooed Kommi's daughter
    his youngest daughter:
'Kommi, give me your daughter
the young maid to be my wife
the just grown to care for me.'
'I'll only give my daughter
to be spouse to Kojo's son
if you shoot a star from heaven
a dot from between the clouds
    raising one arrow

standing on one foot
at a single try.'

And he shot a star from heaven
a dot from between the clouds.
He knocked at Kommi's window
    wooed Kommi's daughter:
'Kommi, give me your daughter
the young maid to be my wife
the just grown to care for me.'
'I'll only give my daughter
to be spouse to Kojo's son
if you walk on needle-points
tread upon iron hatchets
all one day on needle-points
all the next on hatchet-blades.'

He forged footwear of iron
    walked on needle-points
trod upon iron hatchets.
He knocked at Kommi's window
    wooed Kommi's daughter
    his youngest daughter:
'Kommi, give me your daughter
the young maid to be my wife
the just grown to care for me.'
'I'll only give my daughter
to be spouse to Kojo's son
if you swim a stagnant pool
and get from it a great pike—
a great pike with golden scales
    or two smaller ones
and bring it to Kommi's hand
to be mother-in-law's gift.'

Then he swam a stagnant pool
and got from it a great pike—

a great pike with golden scales.
He knocked at Kommi's window
   wooed Kommi's daughter
   his youngest daughter:
'Kommi, give me your daughter!
I've toiled at a thousand tasks
laboured at a hundred more;
   I've swum stagnant pools
   got from there great pike—
   great pike with gold scales
   walked on needle-points
trod upon iron hatchets
   shot a star from heaven
a dot from between the clouds.'
And Kommi gave his daughter—
his daughter, his youngest one
to be spouse to Kojo's son.

That raven, Kojonen's son
grabbed the maid into his sleigh
yanked the bride into the sledge
underneath five woollen cloaks
struck the courser with the lash
whacked it with the beaded tip
   and hurtled away—
drove over swamps, over lands
drove through glades of Väinö-land
over Kalevala's heaths.
Then he much advised the maid
and much he taught the orphan:
'When you come to Kojo's home
   to Kojo's high hill
   fashion woollen skirts
   from one fleece of wool
   and brew barley beer
   from one barley grain.'

They came to a dog's footprints.
The maid sat up in the sleigh
struggles from beneath the quilt:
'What has just run across here?'
'A dog has run across here.'
The maid put this into words:
    'Woe is me, poor wretch!
Better for poor me to be
in a trotting dog's footprints
in the lair of a flop-ear
than in this Kojonen's sledge
under Wrinkle-face's quilt.
    Fairer a dog's hairs
than the curls of Kojo's son.'

That raven, Kojonen's son
twisted his mouth, turned his head
and twisted his black whiskers
struck the courser with the lash
whacked it with the beaded tip
    and hurtled along
    over the clear main
    the open expanse.

They came to a wolf's footprints.
The maid sat up in the sleigh
struggles from beneath the quilt:
'What has just run across here?'
'A wolf has run across here.'
The maid put this into words:
    'Woe is me, poor wretch!
Better for poor me to be
in a veering wolf's footprints
in the steps of a low-snout
than in the raven Kojonen's sledge
under Wrinkle-face's quilt.

Fairer a wolf's hairs
than the curls of Kojo's son.'

That raven, Kojonen's son
twisted his mouth, turned his head
and twisted his black whiskers
struck the courser with the lash
whacked it with the beaded tip
    and hurtled along
over those heaths of the North
through Lapland's gloomy backwoods.

They came to a bear's footprints.
The maid sat up in the sleigh
struggles from beneath the quilt:
'What has just run across here?'
'A bear has run across here.'
The maid put this into words:
    'Woe is me, poor wretch!
Better for poor me to be
in an ambling bear's footprints
the hard roads of a bruin
than in the raven Kojonen's sledge
under Wrinkle-face's quilt.
    Fairer a bear's hairs
than the curls of Kojo's son.'

That raven, Kojonen's son
twisted his mouth, turned his head
and twisted his black whiskers
and he put this into words:
'A little further, stranger
and you'll get to Kojo's home
    to Kojo's high hill;
you'll carve meat without a knife
scoop blood without a ladle.'
When they came to Kojo's home

to Kojo's high hill
he took a sword off a beam
from a peg got a sabre
and asked his sword what it liked
   his sabre for words:
   'Do you eat spare flesh
do you drink blood not needed?'

The sword thought about eating
the sabre said it would drink.
   Then he drew his sword
   and with his brand hacked
the maid into four pieces
into five slices: her head
he pommelled to a hummock
her eyes to swamp cranberries
her hair to dry grass, he carved
her ears for ravens to eat
her flesh he stacked for the birds
her breasts he baked into rolls
her nipples into fish pies—
gifts for the mother-in-law
and presents for Kommi's dame.

He went off to visit her.
Mother-in-law on the hob
   pestered him for news:
   'What news do you know?'
   A serf on a beam
a herdsman on the hob said:
   'Do not ask for news:
   I have had strange dreams.'

The son-in-law gave presents.
Mother eats, is full of praise:
'I've eaten a thing or two—
eaten butter, eaten fat

eaten barren cow
and I've eaten boar
but nothing that tastes like these
gifts from my new son-in-law
    and sent by my child.'

The serf on the beam
the herdsman on the hob said:
'My little flower-footed one
    don't eat the presents!
For if you knew a little
understood a tiny bit
you would surely not eat those
gifts from your new son-in-law
    and sent by your child.'
    'Tell, tell me, poor serf:
what kind of presents are here?'
'If I tell you, poor mistress
you will be washed out with tears
you'll change till you are like mould
sink till you are iron-hued.'
'Let me change though it be much
let me sink though it be twice!
    Tell, tell me, poor serf:
what kind of presents are here?
I'll feed you for one year free
    for two without toil.'
'Now I'll tell you, poor mistress
what kind of presents are there.
'Tis from a woman's arm-bone
bits of Palakainen's* head:
you've eaten your daughter's tits
nipples of your own offspring
her you were long bringing up
suckled at the breast yourself.'

Now she was washed out with tears
she wept one day, she wept two

soon she wept a third as well;
she rolled over at last to
die, changed till she was like mould
sank till she was iron-hued.

The Suitors from the Sea
3:38*

A maid was sitting on sale—
on sale at a rapid's brink
    on a mottled rock
on a fair cliff. All summer
she sat, all the next she wept
waiting for a pleasant man
for a bridegroom with sweet words
a husband to her liking.
From the sea an iron man
rose—iron mouth, iron head
an iron purse in his hand
with iron gifts in a purse:
    'Come to me, poor maid
and marry an iron man!'
'I'll not come, nor do I care:
I was neither meant nor made
    nor brought up at home
to marry an iron man!'
He went back into the sea.

The maid was sitting on sale—
on sale at the rapid's brink
    on the mottled rock
on the fair cliff. All summer
she sat, all the next she wept
waiting for a pleasant man

for a bridegroom with sweet words
a husband to her liking.
From the sea a man of tin
rose—mouth of tin, head of tin
a purse of tin in his hand
with gifts of tin in a purse:
    'Come to me, poor maid
and marry a man of tin!'
'I'll not come, nor do I care:
I was neither meant nor made
    nor brought up at home
to marry a man of tin!'
He went back into the sea.

The maid was sitting on sale—
on sale at the rapid's brink
    on the mottled rock
on the fair cliff. All summer
she sat, all the next she wept
waiting for a pleasant man
for a bridegroom with sweet words
a husband to her liking.
From the sea a copper man
rose—copper mouth, copper head
a copper purse in his hand
with copper gifts in a purse:
    'Come to me, poor maid
and marry a copper man!'
'I'll not come, nor do I care:
I was neither meant nor made
    nor brought up at home
to marry a copper man!'
He went back into the sea.

The maid was sitting on sale—
on sale at the rapid's brink
    on the mottled rock

on the fair cliff. All summer
she sat, all the next she wept
waiting for a pleasant man
for a bridegroom with sweet words
a husband to her liking.
From the sea a man of gold
rose—mouth of gold, head of gold
a purse of gold in his hand
with gifts of gold in a purse:
　　'Come to me, poor maid
and marry a man of gold!'
'I'll not come, nor do I care:
I was neither meant nor made
　　nor brought up at home
to marry a man of gold!'
He went back into the sea.

The maid was sitting on sale—
on sale at the rapid's brink
　　on the mottled rock
on the fair cliff. All summer
she sat, all the next she wept
waiting for a pleasant man
for a bridegroom with sweet words
a husband to her liking.
From the sea a man of bread
rose—mouth of bread, head of bread
a purse of bread in his hand
with gifts of bread in a purse:
　　'Come to me, poor maid
and marry a man of bread!'
　　'Yes, I'll come to you
for I was both meant and made
　　and brought up at home
to marry a man of bread!'

The Ill-Wed
3:40*

A bride wept upon a hill
wallowed on a water-path
   wailed on a well-path
and her father chanced to hear:
'Why are you weeping, my wench
my younger one, why grumbling:
does your father-in-law ill-treat you?'
'Father-in-law treats me well
as my father did at home.'

The bride wept upon the hill
wallowed on the water-path
   wailed on the well-path
and her mother chanced to hear:
'Why are you weeping, my wench
my younger one, why grumbling:
does your mother-in-law ill-treat you?'
'Mother-in-law treats me well
as my mother did at home.'

The bride wept upon the hill
wallowed on the water-path
   wailed on the well-path
and her brother chanced to hear:
'Why are you weeping, sister
my younger one, why grumbling:
does your brother-in-law ill-treat you?'
'Brother-in-law treats me well
as my brother did at home.'

The bride wept upon the hill
wallowed on the water-path

wailed on the well-path
and her sister chanced to hear:
'Why are you weeping, sister
my younger one, why grumbling:
does your sister-in-law ill-treat you?'
'Sister-in-law treats me well
as my sister did at home.'

The bride wept upon the hill
wallowed on the water-path
    wailed on the well-path
and her uncle chanced to hear:
'Why do you weep, brother's girl
my younger one, why grumble:
does your bridegroom ill-treat you?'
'Him, the dog? Yes, he's a dog—
just a dog, son of a dog!
I'd condemn such a bridegroom
to a year's railing in jail
whinnying at the gallows—
I'd condemn him to the beam!
If I saw him being burnt
    I'd stoke up the fire
if I saw him being slashed
I'd put his head on the block
if I saw him being hanged
    I'd pull on the rope.
He turned his back to eat, to
sleep and to do all his work;
nights he took me to his side
    gave me enough arm
and plenty of hateful hand
    his fist raked my hair
    his hand swept my locks.'

The Thoughtful Dragon
3:47*

Let's go to the vale, young ones
us grasshoppers to the cliff
let's cut down a tall lime tree
a lime tree both tall and smooth
pull off a long strip of bast
a strip of bast long and wide
    let's twine a long rope
a rope both long and supple
with which we'll hang the fellow
    hold the woman's son.
Where shall we hang the fellow
    hold the woman's son?
At the road's end, the gatepost
    in the tall doorway
      where the king walks, the
      castle's elder strolls.

The king sternly asks
the castle's elder protests:
    'Why is this man bound
    the woman's son held?'
    This is why he's bound
    the woman's son held:
    he laid a young maid—
    a young maid, a bride.
    The poor maid was doomed
    to the dragon's jaws;
    but the dragon sighed—
    it sighed and it gasped:
    "I'll sooner swallow a young
man, a young man with his sword
or a horse with its saddle

or a priest with his people
or a king with his helmet
than I'll swallow a young maid—
　　a young maid, a bride:
　　a maid will have sons
stow a shipful of children
　　for that mighty war
　　for the well-matched fight
where there's blood up to the knee
heads as many as hummocks."'

The Lost Son
3:54*

A mother has three
sons, a parent three children.
　　One boy went fishing
　　the second hunting
　　the third wolf-trapping.
The first boy came from fishing
and the second from hunting
but no third from wolf-trapping.

　　Who misses the boy?
The mother misses the boy
　　and the mother went
　　to seek her lost son—
ran the wilds as a bruin
as a wolf roamed the backwoods.
Soon when a third night had passed
after a week at the most
　　she climbed a high hill
　　up a lofty peak
shouted from there for her son:

'Where are you, my little boy?
    O my son, come home!'

But from there the boy answers:
'Mother, I cannot get free:
the clouds are holding my head
    the vapours my hair
the rainbows under my arms
and a trap my other foot;
my legs are thrashing at firs
my eyes are counting the stars
before me is a dark cloud
and behind me the clear sky.'

The Foul Maid

3:56*

Two merchants drove, one after
the other across the ice
each on a handsome stallion
    a mouse-coloured horse:
my dad had bought one stallion
    one mouse-coloured horse
and he had bought pretty rings
    and the brightest gifts
for me, a stripling, to wed,
winsome, to go visiting,
    and, handsome, to woo.

Handsome, I went out walking
    and, winsome, wooing.
From the shore I climbed a hill:
there was a house on the hill
    with no way round it

neither up nor down;
I drove into the barnyard
into the little house-yards.
A maid blossomed in the lane
she was decked out at the farm
so I asked, chatted her up:
'Is there a man's wife in you
a bride for a fine fellow?

    Do you know how to
stitch, are you able to sew?'

The maiden indeed answered:
'If I do not know how to
stitch, am not able to sew
    let those who know more
stitch, let the more able sew!
For my mother did not choose
my parents did not allow
a maid to be put on sale
offered in the market square:
tobacco is put on sale
a mare in the market square
but a maid is sold indoors
and traded under a roof.'

Well, that flower-head came indoors
the braid-head under the roofs
and I was amazed: her eyes
had been washed from time to time
her cheeks never in her life
her ears never in this world!

Death on Skis
3:60*

Death was skiing on the swamp
Disease down the winter road.
    Death the great speaks thus
Disease the stout considers
behind the sheds of the house
in the pines below the hill:
'Who shall I kill in the house—
kill the old man in the house?
But if I killed the old man
the fish in the sea would go
with no one to bring them home
and the seines would get tangled
and the nets would drift elsewhere.
No, I'll not kill the old man!'

Death was skiing on the swamp
Disease down the winter road.
    Death the great speaks thus
Disease the stout considers
behind the sheds of the house
in the pines below the hill:
'Who shall I kill in the house—
the old woman in the house?
If I killed the old woman
a snooze on the stove would go
and a broad bum on the bench
a scold in the cabin, a
gossip in the inglenook.
I'll not kill the old woman!'

Death was skiing on the swamp
Disease down the winter road.

Death the great speaks thus
Disease the stout considers
behind the sheds of the house
in the pines below the hill:
'Who shall I kill in the house—
kill the master of the house?
But if I killed the master
the house would be lost, and soon
my little pitch would vanish;
and where then would guests linger
and travelling men abide?
No, I'll not kill my master!'

Death was skiing on the swamp
Disease down the winter road.
    Death the great speaks thus
Disease the stout considers
behind the sheds of the house
in the pines below the hill:
'Who shall I kill in the house—
kill the mistress of the house?
But if I killed the mistress
my pasture would be narrowed
the cow's yield would be cut short
the cups of milk would dry up
the churns of butter would leak.
No, I'll not kill my mistress!'

Death was skiing on the swamp
Disease down the winter road.
    Death the great speaks thus
Disease the stout considers
behind the sheds of the house
in the pines below the hill:
'Who shall I kill in the house—
    shall I kill the son?
    If I killed the son

the clearing-axes would go
the grain-boxes would run down
the plough would fail in the glebe
    buckle in the tilth.
No, I will not kill the son!'

Death was skiing on the swamp
Disease down the winter road.
    Death the great speaks thus
Disease the stout considers
behind the sheds of the house
in the pines below the hill:
'Who shall I kill in the house—
kill the daughter in the house?
But if I killed the daughter
the mouse in the bin would go
and the rat in the larder
suitors would be left grieving
and young boys in bad spirits.
No, I'll not kill the daughter!'

Death was skiing on the swamp
Disease down the winter road.
    Death the great speaks thus
Disease the stout considers
behind the sheds of the house
in the pines below the hill:
'Who shall I kill in the house—
the daughter-in-law? Now, if
I kill the daughter-in-law
the house will not then be lost.
For a wife a wife makes room
one stallion to buy the next;
another wife will be wed
and a mistress will be sought
to live beside the mistress
    knees to hold a son

and a hand to turn a child
like any other mother.'

It killed the daughter-in-law
and got rid of the son's wife.
The man, he weds a new wife
and seeks another mistress
he gets a wife by wedlock
and a mistress by seeking—
but no mother for his child
no nurse for the little wretch
to shove a teat in its mouth
to push a breast in its mouth:
the children were left to cry
the little ones to drip tears.

Paying for the Milk: A Son
3:63*

Lauri, an excellent lad
    fair husband-to-be
    thought this in his mind
    put this into words:
'The happy, the lucky pay
    for their mother's milk
for their mother's blood with cloth
for her labour with velvet.
But poor me, how shall I pay—
how to pay for mamma's milk
make up for mother's torment
for the pains of my parent?
Pay with berries in summer
put right with a catch of fish?
But berries pay for nothing

fish will not make up for much
to offer for mamma's milk
in exchange for mother's pain.
Shoot a grouse on holy ground
a black grouse on berry-ground
or a swan on the river
upon a pool a plump fowl
squirrels on a beam, pick off
a marten on another
and offer them to mother
to my parent for her pains?
But that will not even then
    pay for mother's milk
make up for mamma's torments
no, not for my parent's pains.'

Lauri the excellent lad
    fair husband-to-be
shot a wolf far on the swamp
laid low a bear on the heath
made his mother a fur coat
put silk at collar and cuffs
    trimmed it with broadcloth
the lower part with burlap.
He offered it to mother
    asked her, talked to her:
    'Mummy, old woman
my mamma who carried me
has the milk been paid for now
and the harsh pains made up for?'

    The mother answered
    and spoke for herself:
'No, Larry my little boy
    Lauri my baby
the milk has not been paid for
nor the harsh pains made up for.

You will pay for mamma's milk
the harsh pains of her who nursed
when you build mother a new
cabin, for her who rocked you.'

Lauri the excellent lad
    fair husband-to-be
    built mother a new
cabin, for her who rocked him
    a porch at the front
    two rooms at the back
and he asked her, talked to her:
    'My mum, old woman
has the milk been paid for now
and the harsh pains made up for?'

    The mother answered
    and said with these words:
'No, Larry my little boy
    Lauri my baby
still the milk is not paid for
nor the harsh pains made up for.
You will pay for mamma's milk
the harsh pains of her who nursed
only if you keep mother
nurse mamma in her old age
yourself nurse her who nursed you
carry her who carried you
and stay by her at the end
beside her when life departs
and make a pretty coffin
a narrow room for mother
carry her who carried you
again, borne upon a bier
take your mother to the grave
and fetch mamma to the pit.
Don't fetch her without the priest

but fetch her with the priest's words
with the hollow bell ringing
with the church copper swinging!'

Duke Charles
3:64*

The good lord Duke Charles
Sweden's famous king
strong man in charge of Finland
the fatherland's great master
gets his craft ready
and fits out his ships
prepared the tillers
set them on course for Finland
dressed the tallest masts
on the shoulders of great craft
hoisted the red sails
put up his bright yards.

The craft were ready
the big ships fitted
with their sails of red
green pennants on top.
They came to Finland to war
over waters to battle;
they sailed through the waves
across the billows they drove;
broadly the ships ran
hard those of large size
grimly the boats came
swiftly over the long lakes.
They took a hag for pilot
a Finnish woman to row:

the Finnish woman rowed well
   the boat ran quickly
   ran by the dense hills
beside the solid mountains
edging past the deepest bays
avoiding all the eddies
   skirting the blue rocks
   passing all the cliffs.
   The good lord Duke Charles
the fatherland's great master
strong lord in charge of Finland
saw the land, beheld the shore
   put his craft shoreward
and his vessels at anchor
set the boats on the waters
made fast the ships on the waves
when he came to Turku's lands
   when he reached Finland
   for Finland's great good
the castle's unbidden guest.
He stepped on to the mainland
he sat on Ilponen Hill
   to rest his feet and
   to get his breath back.

He sent word to the castle
   dispatched good news there
conveyed a precious letter
   among Finland's sons
to the halls of great heroes
the cabins of governors
the huts of the town's elders
to the house of the canons.
This is what the letter said
the sound of its precious words:
'I did not come to Finland
   did not come for war

but to make peace, to
reconcile Finland
to break up quarrels
to interrupt fights
to settle the fierce
to turn wrongs to rights.'

The castle's wicked master
evil outcast son
of Turku cobblers
reared by cattle-dogs
bit his lip and wagged his head
and twisted his face
waved his skull about
against Sweden's war.
Harshly harsh he spoke
viciously shameless
he answered bleakly
ill the ill-behaved:
'I'll throw the Duke in the sea
chop up his craft for firewood
smash his boats on the water
his ships for billows to drive!'

The good lord Duke Charles
Sweden's famous king
the fatherland's great master
when he heard the evil news
he advised his knights
to his servants spoke:
'Let us be going
strongly on our way:
to Kupitsa let us walk
let us head for Goosewillow!'

To Kupitsa then they walked
strode to Goosewillow

scrambled up the Turku cliff
    and reached Stable Hill:
to it he moved his great flocks
laid out his camp on the lea
moved a hundred to his flank
another to the other
and a third he placed in front—
fellows with mighty weapons
men of iron on horseback
armoured upon the shoulders.
He landed the equipment
he placed his artillery
transported the copper guns
the brazen horns with effort;
the copper loudly clattered
so did all the brazen horns.
From his tinder-box he took
fire, tackle from his pocket
from his shoulders a hemp cord
    from his belt a fuse
trailed it to the gunpowder
    puts it in the pan
and he let the guns bellow
    the open-throats roar
and the arbalests prattle:
the bullets flew on their way
and the great lead shot travelled
    the long grape-chains creaked
    and hard the sparks hopped
    and smoke poured after.
The guns shrieked on the bulwarks
and the copper drums thudded
badly the wooden pipes shrilled
    the brazen horns blared
stallions neighed, the heath echoed
the cliffs loudly resounded

the shore rang and the sea rocked
and the craft violently shook.

The good lord Duke Charles
the fatherland's great master
shot the castle at random
    up and down the towers
hit a man between the eyes
struck a horse upon the rump:
loudly the best lackeys shrieked
    the lord's servants shrieked
as the castle crumbled, as
    the towers tumbled down.
But when a coward knight leapt
the dust reeked, the ashes stank
mighty lords fled to the swamp
and great masters to the marsh:
Kurki fled among spruces
Arve escaped to the marsh
Hartevik among aspens
Antti scuttled down the road
Sten Finke across the road
to Häme the wicked knight
the plotters to the river
into the steep rapid-foam
    where pike snapped them up
    and perch took their share.

A grey had been got ready
    a clay-hued saddled:
    the good lord Duke Charles
leapt upon the good one's back
and mounted the blaze-brow's rump
gave the hairy-tail its head
let the saddle-back gallop
to below green Viipuri.
Wenches wept in Viipuri

that their boys were gone away
wives in Narva lamented
that their men had been slaughtered.

On Rich and Poor
1887*

Old folk remember
and those today learn
how before their time
life was different here:
without the sun people lived
groped about without the moon
with candles sowing was done
planting performed with torches.
At that time we lived
without the sunshine
without the moonlight stumbled
with our fists fumbled the land
with our hands we sought out roads
with hands roads, with fingers swamps
with candles we ploughed
and furrowed with fire.

Who had covered up our sun
and who had hidden our moon?
Estonian witches covered the sun
German witches hid the moon!
We could not live without sun
nor manage without moonlight;
now, who would seek out the sun
who spy out the moon?
Who else if not God
the one son of God?

The one son of God
Turo the tough, crafty man
    promised he would go
    off to seek the moon
    to spy out the sun.
He wound up a ball of dreams
    took a jug of beer
    an ox horn of mead
thrust a whetstone in his breast
a brush in his shirt front, took
a stallion from the stable
    picked out the best foal
he mounted the black stallion
the horse with the flaxen mane
went off in search of the sun
in pursuit of the moonlight.

He set out along the road
    he rides, he reflects
he rode a mile down the road:
a log lies across the road
across and along the road
and he can't get past the log
he could not go over it
neither over nor under
nor could birds fly over it
nor could worms crawl under it.
Turo the tough, crafty man
took some beer out of the jug
some mead out of the ox horn
    splashed the beer on it
    and sprinkled his mead:
    the log split in two
an eternal road appeared
a track ancient as iron
    for the great, the small
    the middling to tread.

He went on a little way
he rode a mile down the road:
a hill lies across the road
across and along the road
and he can't get over it
cannot escape around it;
many men, many horses
are rotting under the hill.
Turo the tough, crafty man
looked some beer out of the jug
some mead out of the ox horn
    spilled the mead on it
    and he splashed his beer:
    the hill fell in two
an eternal road was born
a track ancient as iron
    for the great, the small
    the middling to tread.

He rode on a little way
he did a mile down the road
and he comes upon a sea:
the sea lies across the road
and he can't get over it
cannot escape around it;
many men, many horses
cover the shore with their bones.
Turo the tough, crafty man
took some beer out of his jug
some mead out of the ox horn
    splashed the beer on it
    and sprinkled his mead;
but the sea would not heed that
so he said a word or two:
    the sea broke in two
an eternal road appeared
a track ancient as iron

for the young, the old
for middle-aged to stroll.

He rode on a little way
kept on down the road a bit
and the Demon's cabins loom
and the Demon's roofs glimmer;
there is one shed on a hill
and three maidens in the shed
    are scouring the moon
    and washing the sun.
Turo the tough, crafty man
    saw the moon gleaming
    and the sun shining
and he stepped to the shed door
    takes the ball of dreams
    lobbed the ball of dreams
    at the Demon's maids
and he got the maids to sleep.
    He shouldered the moon
put the sun upon his head
and sets off for his own lands
    for his homelands bound.

He rode on a little way
he did a mile down the road
and hears a rumbling behind
    so he glances back:
they are coming to catch him
    and to seize him fast.
Turo the tough, crafty man
took the whetstone from his breast
and tossed it from his shirt front
    before the pursuers:
    'Let a thick rock grow
    a thick, heavy rock

so they can't get over it
　　over or round it!'

Turo the tough, crafty man
　　rides forward from there
　　made a day's journey
and a rumbling follows him
　　so he glances back:
the Demon with his dread band
is again coming to catch
　　and to seize him fast.
Turo the tough, crafty man
took the brush out of his breast
and tossed it from his shirt front
　　before the pursuers:
　　'Let a spruce wood grow
with iron boughs on the trees
　　so they cannot go
　　through it or past it!'
　　There a spruce wood grew
with iron boughs on the trees
　　and they cannot go
　　through it or past it.

Turo the tough, crafty man
　　came to his own lands
and brought the sun as he came
and with him conveyed the moon
and he put the sun to shine
the sunlight to make merry
　　in a gold-topped spruce
　　on the highest boughs
and the moon he raised to gleam
at the top of a tall pine:
　　the sun shone brightly
　　from the highest boughs
shone upon those with fathers

    the rich, the happy
but not on the fatherless
    the poor, the hapless.

Turo the tough, crafty man
took the sun from where it shone
    from the highest boughs
    to the lowest boughs:
    the sun shone clearly
    from the lowest boughs
shone upon the fatherless
the troubled, those full of care
but not on those with fathers
    not on the lucky.

Turo the tough, crafty man
moved the sun from where it shone
from the lowest boughs to those
in the middle of the tree:
now the sun shone equally
on the rich and on the poor
shone upon those with fathers
    the rich, the cherished
and upon the fatherless
    the poor, the beggars;
and merrily the sun shone
    sweetly the moon gleamed
on the doors of the lucky
on the thresholds of the poor.

NOTES

iv Though the victim is different, this ballad is clearly related to the Scottish 'Edward, Edward', No. 61 in *The Oxford Book of Ballads*, ed. James Kinsley (1969). The tune of 'The Brother-Slayer' is the fifth of six *Finnish Folk Tunes* for piano by Sibelius (1903).

xix *her love's ship*: with a red sail.

1:1 *music*: here, as throughout the tradition, the Finnish word (*soitto*) also means 'musical instrument'.

Väinämöinen (*ä* like *a* in 'hat', *ö* as in German, first syllable stress always): the demigod hero of the *Kalevala*, who in canto 40 makes the first kantele from the bones of a giant pike. This opening lyric, composed by Lönnrot from folk sources, like the *Kalevala* prologue and epilogue, discredits the epic account, which identifies music with joy.

1:4 Cf. *Kalevala* 25:429 ff.

hay-shod: wearing birchbark shoes stuffed with hay to keep out the cold.

bark bread: in times of hardship dough was supplemented with pine cambium, the tissue between the bark and the wood.

1:6 *throat-trump*: the image is based on a *torvi*, a herdsman's trump or horn of birchbark strips wound into a long cone.

burnt ground: a clearing made by burning scrub, which is then dug in for fertilizer.

a felled pine: the harrow.

1:12 *he*: or 'she' throughout the book when sex is not otherwise marked. Finnish has no grammatical gender.

farthing: money was rare in the bards' world, so its terms are used arbitrarily. Here, 'farthing' renders *äyri* (from Swedish *öre*), 'penny' *riuna* (from Russian *grivna*, *grivennik*, a 10 kopek piece), 'shilling' *kopeikka*.

1:23 *Thomas*: the feast of St Thomas, 21 December.

All Saints: **kekri**, originally a Karelian festival named after a guardian spirit of livestock and crops. 1 November was additionally important because it was when servants hired for a year could change employers.

1:25 Cf. *Kalevala* 4:197 ff., 22:173 ff.

calloos: Scottish name of the long-tailed duck (*Clangula hyemalis*), associated in Finnish tradition with sorrow.

1:46 Cf. *Kalevala* 4:217 ff., 35:279 ff.

verses: in modern Finnish *luku* here would mean 'chapter', but the word still has the vagueness of its origin in an unlettered society and can refer to many things counted, read, or recited. Cf. 2:20.

1:54 Cf. *Kalevala* 22:439 ff.

castles: literally 'Viipuris', after the Baltic port. See note to 1:117.

1:57 Cf. *Kalevala* 5:200 ff., 21:345 ff. Set by Sibelius as the seventh of *Nine Part-Songs*, Op. 18.

1:61 Cf. *Kalevala* 4:507 ff.

1:72 Cf. *Kalevala* 34:77 ff.

song-leader: rendering *virsiporras*, the lead singer of a pair (men) or group (women) in traditional performance. The term is metaphorical, *porras* meaning a stair, or a plank across a swamp or stream. The poem plays on the metaphor.

1:108 Apparently a popular re-creation of a poem printed in 1777 in response to a law passed in the reign of the Swedish King Gustav III banning the home manufacture of spirit alcohol.

above the smoke-line: sitting on top of the traditional stone stove rather than at table.

1:110 Cf. *Kalevala* 20:139 ff. A lyric version of the epic recipe, with birds instead of spirits.

Origin: rendering *synty* 'birth', in spells a recitation of a thing's imagined origin, in order to have power over it.

Osma's . . . Kaleva's: referring to obscure mythological ancestors. Kalevala is Kaleva-land.

1:117 Cf. *FFPE* 110.

Viipuri: port north-west of St Petersburg (Leningrad); since 1945 Vyborg, USSR.

Narva: port in north-east Estonia.

1:122 Set by Sibelius as the third and final movement of *Rakastava* ('The Lover'), Op. 14. He omits the sections beginning 'Kneel down', 'That's all' and 'Get up'.

1:134 Cf. *Kalevala* 24:187 ff.

1:144 Cf. *Kalevala* 24:367 ff.

1:160 Cf. *Kalevala* 11:385 ff., which is spoken by Lemminkäinen's mother to persuade him to give up raiding.

cowberry: *Vaccinium vitis-idaea*, a kind of bilberry.

Savo: province of central Finland adjoining Karelia.

blue . . . red . . . white paper: Imperial Russian 5, 10, and 25 rouble notes.

1:173–4 Set by Sibelius as the first two movements of *Rakastava*.

1:186 Set by Sibelius as the third of the *Nine Part-Songs*.

1:219 Set by Sibelius as the fourth of the *Nine Part-Songs*.

bath-whisk: the accepted but misleading English equivalent for leafy birch twigs used to stimulate sweat in the sauna.

2:31 *honey-berry*: a literal rendering of *mesimarja*, since both elements connote affection. Otherwise *mesimarja* is Arctic bramble (*Rubus arcticus*), from which a liqueur is made.

2:43 A variant of this poem was first printed in A. F. Skjöldebrand, *Voyage pittoresque au Cap Nord* (Stockholm, 1801) and Joseph Acerbi, *Travels through Sweden, Finland, and Lapland to the North Cape, in the years 1798 and 1799* (London, 1802), with French and English literal versions respectively; the first verse translation was Goethe's *Finnisches Lied* (1810). This is discussed, with the 'original' and an English verse translation, in the introduction to my translation of the *Kalevala*. Of the 'chanson, composée par une simple paysanne finoise [*sic*]', 70 variants have since been found. In the *Kanteletar*, Lönnrot gives two texts, the second of which is translated here.

2:53 Cf. *Kalevala* 37:19 ff.

2:55 *kiln*: *riihi*, a building where grain was dried in mild heat and threshed.

2:121 Cf. *Kalevala* 4.

2:123 Cf. *Kalevala* 36:307 ff.

2:124 Cf. *Kalevala* 4:197 ff.

2:137 Cf. *Kalevala* 23:519 ff.

2:154 Cf. 3:63 'Paying for the Milk: A Son'. Here the daughter knows that on marrying she will live with her husband's family.

   her labour: literally 'her sauna-path' (*saunatiensä*). The sauna was the usual place for confinements.

   birch sap: a healthy drink, now sold in health-food shops.

2:155 *serf for a year*: therefore, strictly, a hired man, who had the right to change employers. Serfs, generally unknown in Finland, had no such right.

2:171 Cf. *Kalevala* 23:617 ff.

   brake: flax was braked (crushed) in the sauna.

   club: for pounding laundry.

2:174 *tin*: the semiprecious metal was used for adornment.

2:186 *burn*: see note to 1:6 *burnt ground*.

2:195 *Tornio*: northernmost port of the Gulf of Bothnia between Finland and Sweden.

   rix-dollars: *riksi*, from Dutch *rijksdaler*, an international silver coin in use from the 17th century to the mid-19th. (The Spanish version was the 'piece of eight' of adventure stories; the figure 8—*reales*—evolved into the American dollar sign.)

2:209 The earliest printed variant of this poem (1778) is a grinding song in which the bard wanders from theme to theme as she works. The 'Cripple's Wife' theme occupies only the first 15 lines; then comes a 4-line echo of 'Missing Him' (2:43), which modulates into 24 lines of 'Elegy'

material (2:53), and the variant ends—for good measure—with 6 lines on the 'Irresistible' theme (2:50).

2:220 Cf. *Kalevala* 31:1 ff.

2:258 *Finland . . . Karelia*: 'Finland' is probably Häme, the
southern region around Lake Päijänne; the Islands are
Ahvenanmaa (Swedish Åland), off the south-west coast;
Ostrobothnia is the central coastal region; Savo is the
central region adjoining Karelia, which straddles the
Finnish–Russian border, whence 'both halves'.

2:261 Cf. *Kalevala* 19:78 ff., 26:633 ff. The snake image is
more explicitly sexual here.

2:265 Cf. *Kalevala* 36:25 ff.

2:271 Cf. *Kalevala* 1:1 ff., 25:413 ff.

Dreamer: rendering *Unta*, also *Untamo*, perhaps an
obscure buried shaman who has 'strayed here from the
epic poems' (Julius Krohn). In *Kalevala* 5:17 ff., the
shaman Väinämöinen asks his shade where mermaids are
to be found. The name resembles—and may be related
to—*uni* 'sleep, dream'.

2:283 *cairns*: *raunio* (modern Finnish 'ruin') was a pile of
stones left after ploughing, the original meaning of the
English word (from Celtic).

rye puddings: rendering *mämmikakkara*. *Mämmi* is a baked
pudding of rye meal, malt, and water, traditionally eaten
at Easter; *kakkara*, a small cake or bun, can only mean a
portion here.

2:327 *Old Man*: *Ukko*, the chief god in old Finnish myth. Cf.
modern Finnish *ukko* 'old man', *ukkonen* 'thunder'.

God: *Jumala*, another name of *Ukko* (cf. Lappish *jubmel*
'sky, heaven'), adopted by Christianity for 'God'.

2:329 Cf. *Kalevala* 46 and 14.

2:333 Cf. *Kalevala* 14.

2:350 Cf. *Kalevala* 46:87 ff., 499 ff.

3:4 Cf. *FFPE* 77–9. Probably based on the parable of Dives
and Lazarus (Luke 16:19–31); cf. 'Dives and Lazarus',
No. 3 in the Kinsley *Oxford Book of Ballads*. As Lönnrot's

title *Viron orja ja isäntä* ('The Estonian Serf and Master')
shows, the setting is Estonia, whose language and culture
are closely related to Finland's and whose serfdom (under
German landlords) was notorious. Oddly, the first four
lines are rhyming couplets.

3:6 Cf. *Kalevala* 50 and *FFPE* 59–63. The legends are
numbered in the present translation, though not in the
Finnish. (i) Mary becomes pregnant from swallowing a
berry (*marja*); her Finnish name *Maaria* appears some-
times as Marjatta, the *Kalevala* form. (ii) Her mother
turns her out; she seeks and finds a sauna, where she gives
birth to God. (iii) Stephen, Herod's stable-lad, leaves his
master on seeing the star of Bethlehem. (iv) Mary's child
disappears, an echo of Luke 2: 41–51 (and less of a jolt
than at *Kalevala* 50:351) that leads straight to his death.
(v) After God's death, Mary arranges his resurrection and
the disordered world returns to normal. (vi) God tricks
Judas (Satan) into the shackles Judas has forged for him,
and ascends to heaven.

(ii) *Saraja* (*j* as in 'hallelujah'): a mythical place-name,
appearing in the *Kalevala* also as *Saraoja* ('Sedgeditch')
and Sariola, alias Northland (*Pohjola*).

gipsy: *kasakka*, an itinerant worker, popularly supposed
to be of Cossack origin, as English gipsies were thought
to hail from Egypt, whence their name. Not the same as
the Finnish Romany, *mustalaiset* ('the swarthy ones'), who
do not figure in the tradition.

(iii) The Finnish legend of Stephen bears little relation to
the account of the First Martyr in Acts 6–7. His associ-
ation with horses seems to be due to his feast (27
December in Orthodoxy) falling nearer than any other
major saint's to the winter solstice, when horses were
ritually watered for luck; a folk memory of this practice
may survive as the Boxing Day race meeting. Other
elements of the legend derive from many sources, not
always invoking Stephen. The roast cock that crows is
part of the English Christmas, thanks to 'King Herod and
the Cock', No. 54 in *The Oxford Book of Carols*, where it
is the Wise Men, as in the Gospel, not Stephen, who tell

Herod about Jesus; a footnote traces the legend to a 12th-century Danish ballad. It also occurs in a 15th-century Greek MS of the apocryphal Gospel of Nicodemus, or Acts of Pilate: Judas tells his wife that he is going to hang himself, but she replies that Jesus's resurrection is as unlikely to happen as 'this cock that is roasting on the fire of coals can crow', which it then does. An English ballad MS of the same century, No. 2 in Kinsley, also has a roast cock crowing, but in circumstances similar to the Finnish. Stephen, a 'clerk', tells Herod he is leaving him to follow Jesus, whereupon Herod declares that if Jesus is so special the capon in his dish will crow: 'That word was not so sone seyd, / That word in that halle, / The capoun crew *Christus natus est* / Among the lordes alle.' The ballad ends with Herod ordering his 'turmentowres' to stone Stephen, as in Acts 7; but the Finnish bards felt no such obligation to Scripture.

(vi) 'Then the King of glory took hold upon the head of the chief ruler Satan, and delivered him unto the angels and said: Bind down with irons his hands and his feet and his neck and his mouth. And then he delivered him unto Hades, saying: Take him and keep him safely until my second coming' (from the Greek version of the Descent into Hell, attached to the Gospel of Nicodemus, or Acts of Pilate; in M. R. James (ed. and trans.), *The Apocryphal New Testament*, Oxford, 1924). Such texts, derived from Revelation 20, correspond in Orthodox tradition to the Harrowing of Hell, much depicted in medieval Western art and literature. This occurred between the Crucifixion and the Resurrection, according to the Apostles' Creed, which is used only in the West; it is not mentioned in the Nicene Creed. Orthodoxy associates the Descent with the Ascension, as implied in Ephesians 4: 'Now that he ascended, what is it but that he also descended first into the lower parts of the earth?'

Judas: Finnish tradition identifies him not only with Satan but with Hiisi, a forest demon associated with metalworking and noise; cf. English 'pandemonium'. The connection between devilry and noise is often made on the grounds that the latter interferes with worship and

study. A further connection, between Jews and metalworking, lurks in the bowels of Christian exegesis: since
God banned the use of iron tools in building the first altar
in the promised land (Deut. 27) and Solomon's temple
(1 Kings 6), the Jews have only themselves to blame for
the consequences of having Jesus nailed to the cross.

3:7 Cf. *FFPE* 66–7. Based on the oldest MS (*c.*1671) in the
folklore archives of the Finnish Literature Society, this
poem was composed—perhaps in the late 13th century—
in western Finland, where the events described took
place. In 1155 (or 1154) King Eric Jedvardsson ('the
Good') of Sweden and Bishop Henry of Uppsala, apparently an Englishman, brought Christianity—and Swedish
rule—to Finland. The poem tells of the martyrdom in
1156 of Henry by a murderer he had tried to bring to
justice.

Cabbageland: rendering *Kaalimaa*, now read literally
(*kaali* 'cabbage', *maa* 'land') as the country where cabbage
was a staple food, apparently England; some MSS actually
state that Henry was born in England. (see frontispiece)

no ice: in winter they could drive straight across the ice,
so this must be early spring. Cf. the 'winter road' across a
frozen swamp in 3:60.

Kiulo: a dialect form of Köyliö, a lake near Turku.

3:8 Cf. *FFPE* 84. The dialogue suggests a sophisticated
author and perhaps dramatic performance: one MS is set
out as a play, another divides the poem into five scenes.
The present translation is similarly divided, though the
Finnish is not. The villain of the piece, Klaus Kurki,
merges two men—Klaus Kurki, lord of Laukko from
1450 till 1470, a district judge who tried to stamp out
witchcraft (referred to near the end of the second 'scene');
and Klaus Djäkn, another district judge, who burnt his
wife to death and married a woman called Kristina (Kirsti)
at least 50 years before. (Because the ballad is from
western Finland, the names *Uolevi* and *Uoti* have been
rendered Olaf and Wat.)

3:10 Cf. *FFPE* 145. History suffers a sea-change in oral

tradition. This ballad, based on material widespread throughout Russian Karelia, combines three tsars laying four sieges to three castles (one Finnish, two Latvian) with a Swedish castle-lord who lived later than most of the events: 'Matti son of Lauri' can at least be identified as Mats Larsson Kruse, who was made 'master of Viipuri' in 1583. The story-teller is a loyal Finnish subject of the tsar, who regards Swedes (including most Finns, since Finland was part of Sweden till 1809) as barbarians and heretics. Out of all this comes a poem about Sweden's loss to Russia of Viipuri. Founded by Sweden in the 13th century, the former Hanseatic port was Russian from 1721 till 1812.

Volmari: Valmiera, a fortified town north-east of Riga.

3:15 Cf. *Kalevala* 4, 36:323 ff.; *FFPE* 104–5.

3:16 Cf. *FFPE* 95–6. The latter, collected from an Ingrian woman in 1883, expands the 'lyrical epic' element with dialogue between the murderer and his children. He tells them he will bring them a better mother, but they reply: 'You'll not bring us a mother / you'll bring a wife for yourself / you'll bring us one who tears hair / who shares hair out to the wind / gives it to the gale . . .'

mistress: of the household, as throughout.

3:25 Cf. *FFPE* 7, 18–20. Episodes with parallels in the *Kalevala* are: the maid's complaint (11:238 ff.), the suitor's second task (17:11 ff.), the 'journey' formula (e.g. 10:7 ff.), the advice about housework (10:259 ff., the Sampo recipe), the animal footprints (38:179 ff.), the dialogue with the sword (36:319 ff.), the tasty titbit (17:105 ff.).

Swanlike: *jouten*, literally 'idle', but there is a pun here with *joutsen* 'swan'; cf. English slang 'to swan'. The implication seems to be that a girl who marries in hopes of an easy life is heading for trouble.

Palakainen's: from Russian Pelagiya, but the Finnish name also has grisly overtones of *pala(nen)* 'titbit'.

3:38 Cf. *FFPE* 111–12; 115 is a parody, in which the success-
ful suitor is a thief.

3:40 Cf. *FFPE* 122–3. For the closing lines, cf. *Kalevala*
23:649–50, 717 ff.

3:47 Cf. *FFPE* 72–4.

3:54 Cf. *FFPE* 129–31.

3:56 A parody of wedding ritual (cf. 1:160). By 1898, when
FFPE 114 was collected, the humour had got rougher:
the girl's family are 'snub-noses' and 'farters', and the girl
herself has 'eyes . . . deep in pig-muck / and her ears in
dog-slobber'.

3:60 Cf. *FFPE* 80–1.

3:63 Cf. 2:154, 'Paying for the Milk: A Daughter', and *FFPE*
100, which has a happier—if less convincing—ending.

3:64 Cf. *FFPE* 143. Like 'The Pan under Arrest' (1:108),
this poem does not derive from oral tradition: it is
propaganda composed in oral style. It concerns the efforts
of the future Charles IX of Sweden to assert his power
against King Sigismund of Poland, who at the end of the
16th century sought to annexe Sweden–Finland. The
ballad reflects Finnish support for Charles, called 'precious' in an early 18th-century MS, but only 'famous'
here.

1887 Cf. *FFPE* 32–3, and see Appendix.

APPENDIX

FINNISH TEXT OF
'ON RICH AND POOR'

Turo, kuun ja auringon pelastaja

Väki vanha muistelevi,
Nykyinen opetteleikse,
Kuink' on ennen aikoinansa
Toisin täällä toimiteltu,
Ilman päivättä eletty,
Kupaeltu kuutamotta,
Kynttelillä kylvö tehty,
Touko pantu tuohuksilla.
  Elettynä on ennen meillä
Ilman päivän valkeuetta,
Kuun valotta kupsittuna,
Kourin maita koiteltuna,
Käsin teitä etsittynä,
Käsin teitä, sormin soita;
Kynttelillä kynnettynä,
Vaottuna valkealla.
  Ken se meiltä päivän peitti,
Kuka meiltä kuun salasi?—
Viron noiat päivän peitti,
Saksan noiat kuun salasi.
  Voitu ei päivättä elä'ä,
Kuun valotta kupsaella;
Kenpä päivän etsijäksi,
Kuka kuun tähystäjäksi?—
Kukas muu kuin ei Jumala,
Jumalaisen aino poika.
  Jumalaisen aino poika,
Turo tuima, mies kavala,
Lähteäksensä käkesi,
Mennä kuuta etsimähän,
Päivä'ä tähyämähän.
  Kerivi kerälle unta,

Otti kannusen olutta,
Härän sarvisen metoa,
Pisti sieran seslehensä,
Harjan paitansa povehen;
Otti tallista orosen,
Valitsi parahan varsan,
Istui mustalle orolle,
Liinaharjalle hevolle,
Läksi päivän etsintähän,
Kuutamon tavotantahan.
  Alkoi mennä tietä myöten,
Ajavi, ajattelevi,
Ajoi tietä virstan verran,
Hako on tiellä poikkipuolin,
Poikin tietä, pitkin tietä,
Ei pääse haon sivutse,
Ei voinut ylitse mennä,
Ei ylitse, ei alatse,
Pääse ei linnut lentäväiset,
Ei maot matelevaiset.
  Turo tuima, mies kavala,
Otti kannusta olutta,
Härän sarvesta metoja,
Läikähytteli olutta,
Metostansa tilkahutti,
Hako halkesi kaheksi,
Tuli tie ijän ikuinen,
Rata rauan polvuhinen,
Käy suuren, käyä pienen,
Käy keskinkertahisen.
  Meni matka'a vähäisen,
Ajoi tietä virstan verran,

Mäki on tiellä poikkipuolin,
Poikin tietä, pitkin tietä,
Ei pääse mäen ylitse,
Ei voi ympäri paeta;
Moni mies, moni hevonen,
Alla mäen märkänevät.
      Turo tuima, mies kavala,
Katsoi kannusta olutta,
Härän sarvesta metoa,
Tipahutteli metoa,
Oluttansa läikähytti,
Mäki kahtehen katosi,
Tie syntyi ijän ikuinen,
Rata rauan polvuhinen,
Käyä suuren, käyä pienen,
Käyä keskinkertahisen.
      Ajoi matka'a vähäisen,
Teki tietä virstan verran,
Meri vastahan tulevi,
Meri tiellä poikinpuolin,
Ei pääse meren ylitse,
Ei voi ympäri paeta;
Moni mies, moni hevonen,
Peitti rannan raaoillansa.
      Turo tuima, mies kavala,
Otti kannusta olutta,
Härän sarvesta metoa,
Läikähytteli olutta,
Metostansa tilkahutti,
Ei tuosta meri totellut,
Niin sanoi pari sana'a,
Meri kahtia hajosi,
Tie tuli ijän ikuinen,
Rata rauan polvuhinen,
Käyä nuoren, käyä vanhan,
Keiketellä kesk'ikäisen.
      Ajoi matka'a vähäisen,
Piti tietä pikkaraisen,
Hiien huonehet näkyvät,
Katot Hiien kaljottavat.
      Yks' on aittanen mäellä,
Kolme neittä aittasessa,

Nuopa kuuta kuura'avat,
Sekä päivyttä pesevät.
      Turo tuima, mies kavala,
Näki kuun kumottavaksi,
Sekä päivän paistavaksi,
Astui aittasen ovelle,
Ottavi unikeräsen,
Niin viskoi unikeräsen
Päälle Hiien neiokkaisten,
Saatti neiot nukkumahan.
      Otti kuuhuen olalle,
Pani päivän päänsä päälle,
Lähtevi omille maille,
Kotimaille kulkemahan.
      Ajoi matka'a vähäisen,
Teki tietä virstan verran,
Kuulevi kumun perästä,
Niin taaksensa katsahtavi:
Ollahan tavottamassa,
Aivan kiinni ottamassa.
      Turo tuima, mies kavala,
Otti sieran seslestähän,
Viskoi paitansa povesta
Etehen ahistajille:
„Kasvakohon paasi paksu,
Paasi paksu ja järeä,
Ett' eivät ylitse pääse,
Ei ylitse, ympäritse!"
      Turo tuima, mies kavala,
Tuosta eellehen ajavi,
Teki tietä päiväyksen,
Kuuluvi kumu jälestä,
Niin taaksensa katsahtavi:
Hiisi hirmujoukkoinensa
Taas ompi tapa'amassa,
Aivan kiinni ottamassa.
      Turo tuima, mies kavala,
Otti harjan seslestänsä,
Viskoi paitansa povesta,
Etehen ahistajille:
„Kasvakohon kuusikorpi,
Rauta-oksat kuusosihin,

Jott' ei pääse kulkemahan
Ei lävitse, ei sivutse!"
  Kasvoi tuohon kuusikorpi,
Rauta-oksat kuusosihin,
Eivät pääse kulkemahan,
Ei lävitse, ei sivutse.
  Turo tuima, mies kavala,
Jo tuli omille maille,
Toi on päivän tullessansa,
Kerallansa kuun kuletti.
  Pani päivän paistamahan,
Auringon iloitsemahan,
Kultalatva kuusosehen,
Oksille ylimmäisille,
Kuun nosti kumottamahan
Pitkän latvahan petäjän.
  Päivä paistoi kirkkahasti
Oksilta ylimmäisiltä,
Se paistoi isällisille,
Rikkahille, riemuisille,
Ei paista isättömille,
Köyhille, surullisille.
  Turo tuima, mies kavala,

Otti päivän paistamasta
Oksilta ylimmäisiltä
Oksille alimmaisille:
Päivä paistoi kimmeästi,
Oksilta alimmaisilta,
Se paistoi isättömille,
Vaivaisille, huoleisille,
Ei paista isällisille,
Ei onnen osallisille.
  Turo tuima, mies kavala,
Siirsi päivän paistamasta
Oksilta alimmaisilta
Oksille keskellä puuta.
Niin päivä tasoin paistoi
Köyhille ja rikkahille,
Se paistoi isällisille,
Rikkahille, rakkahille,
Ja paistoi isättömille,
Köyhille, kerä'äjille,
Iloisesti päivä paistoi,
Suloisesti kuu kumotti,
Osallisien oville,
Kansan köyhän kynnyksille.